"Interesting seeing you again, Ryan," Jaci said in a catch-a-clue voice.

A puzzled frown pulled his brows together. "Maybe we should have coffee, catch up."

"Honey, you don't even know who I am, so what, exactly, would be the point? Goodbye, Ryan."

"Okay, busted. So who are you?" Ryan roughly demanded. "I know that I know you..."

"You'll work it out," Jaci told him and heard him utter a low curse as she walked away. But she wasn't sure if he would connect her with the long-ago teenager who'd hung on his every word. She doubted it. There was no hint of the insecure girl she used to be...on the outside anyway. Besides it would be fun to see his face when he realized that she was Neil's sister, the woman Neil wanted him to help navigate the "perils" of New York City.

"Then how about another kiss to jog my memory?" Ryan called out just as she was about to walk into the ballroom.

She turned around slowly and tipped her head to the side. "Let me think about that for a minute...mmm...no."

But hot damn, Jaci thought as she walked off, she was tempted.

Dear Reader,

This is my first outing for Harlequin Desire and I am properly excited to be part of this wonderful series!

For this book, I really wanted to explore how much impact a single kiss can have, and when Jaci kisses Ryan to get rid of a very persistent, toad-like billionaire who is determined to see her naked, she sets in motion a series of events that even I had trouble keeping up with.

Ryan turns out to be Jaci's new boss, and the toady billionaire is Ryan's investor in his movie. Ryan and Jaci have to fake a relationship to keep the client happy. And then there's the hectic chemical reaction the two of them generate whenever they are in the same room. Neither Jaci nor Ryan is looking for love; they are both antirelationship for different reasons and quite resistant to commitment. I had to make them work for their happily-ever-after!

A book is not really a book until it's in the hands of the reader. So, thank you for reading mine. I hope you enjoy Ryan and Jaci's story as much as I enjoyed writing about them.

Happy reading and best wishes,

Joss

Facebook: Joss Wood Author

Twitter: @josswoodbooks

TAKING THE BOSS TO BED

—

JOSS WOOD

H HARLEQUIN® DESIRE

Recycling programs
for this product may
not exist in your area.

ISBN-13: 978-0-373-73431-3

Taking the Boss to Bed

Copyright © 2015 by Joss Wood

Printed in U.S.A.

HARLEQUIN®
www.Harlequin.com

Joss Wood wrote her first book at the age of eight and has never really stopped writing. Her passion for putting letters on a blank screen is matched only by her love of books and traveling—especially to the wild places of Southern Africa—and possibly by her hatred of ironing and making school lunches.

Fueled by coffee, when she's not writing or being a hands-on mum, Joss—with her background in business and marketing—works for a nonprofit organization to promote the local economic development and collective business interests of the area where she resides. Happily and chaotically surrounded by books, family and friends, she lives in KwaZulu-Natal, South Africa, with her husband, children and their many pets.

Books by Joss Wood

Harlequin Desire

Taking the Boss to Bed

Harlequin Kiss

The Last Guy She Should Call
Flirting with the Forbidden
More Than a Fling?
Your Bed or Mine?
The Honeymoon Arrangement

Visit her Author Profile page at Harlequin.com, or josswoodbooks.wordpress.com, for more titles.

One

Jaci Brookes-Lyon walked across the art deco, ridiculously ornate lobby of the iconic Forrester-Grantham Hotel on Park Avenue to the bank of elevators flanked by life-size statues of 1930s cabaret dancers striking dance poses. She stopped next to one, touching the smooth, cool shoulder with her fingertips.

Sighing through pursed lips, she looked at the dark-eyed blonde staring back at her in the supershiny surface of the elevator doors in front of her. Short, layered hair in a modern pixie cut, classic, fitted cocktail dress, perfect makeup, elegant heels. She looked good, Jaci admitted. Sophisticated, assured and confident. Maybe a tad sedate but that could be easily changed.

What was important was that the mask was in place. She looked like the better, stronger, New York version of herself, the person she wanted to be. She appeared to be someone who knew where she was going and how she was going to get there. Pity, Jaci thought, as she pushed her long bangs out of a smoky eye, that the image was still as substantial as a hologram.

Jaci left the elevator and took a deep breath as she walked across the foyer to the imposing double doors of the ballroom. *Here goes*, she thought. Stepping into the room packed with designer-dressed men and women, she reminded herself to put a smile on her face and to keep her spine straight. Nobody had to know that she'd rather stroll around Piccadilly Circus naked than walk into a room filled with people she didn't know. Her colleagues from Starfish were here somewhere. She'd sat with them earlier through the interminably long awards ceremony. Her new friends, Wes and Shona, fellow writers employed by Starfish, had promised to keep her company at her first film industry after-party, and once she found them she'd be fine. Between now and then, she just had to look as if she was having fun or, at the very least, happy to be surrounded by handsome men and supersophisticated women. Dear Lord, was that Candice Bloom, the multiple Best Actress award winner? Was it unkind to think that she looked older and, dare she even think it, fatter in real life?

Jaci took a glass of champagne from a tray that wafted past her and raised the glass for a taste. Then she clutched it to her chest and retreated to the side of the room, keeping an eye out for her coworkers. If she hadn't found them in twenty minutes she was out of there. She spent her entire life being a wallflower at her parents' soirees, balls and dinner parties, and had no intention of repeating the past.

"That ring looks like an excellent example of Georgian craftsmanship."

Jaci turned at the voice at her elbow and looked down into the sludge-brown eyes of the man who'd stepped up to her side. Jaci blinked at his emerald tuxedo and thought that he looked like a frog in a shiny suit. His thin black hair was pulled back off his forehead and was gathered at his neck in an oily tail, and he sported a silly soul patch under his thin, cruel mouth.

Jaci Brookes-Lyon, magnet for creepy guys, she thought.

He picked up her hand to look at her ring. Jaci tried to tug it away but his grip was, for an amphibian, surprisingly strong. "Ah, as I thought. It's an oval-faceted amethyst, foiled and claw-set with, I imagine, a closed back. The amethyst is pink and lilac. Exquisite. The two diamonds are old, mid-eighteenth century."

She didn't need this dodgy man to tell her about her ring, and she pulled her hand away, resisting the urge to wipe it on her cinnamon-shaded cocktail dress. Ugh. Creep factor: ten thousand.

"Where did you get the ring?" he demanded, and she caught a flash of dirty, yellow teeth.

"It's a family heirloom," Jaci answered, society manners too deeply ingrained just to walk off and leave him standing there.

"Are you from England? I love your accent."

"Yes."

"I have a mansion in the Cotswolds. In the village Arlingham. Do you know it?"

She did, but she wouldn't tell him that. She'd never manage to get rid of him then. "Sorry, I don't. Would you exc—"

"I have a particularly fine yellow diamond pendant that would look amazing in your cleavage. I can just imagine you wearing that and a pair of gold high heels."

Jaci shuddered and ruthlessly held down a heave as he ran his tongue over his lips. Seriously? Did that pickup line ever work? She picked his hand off her hip and quickly dropped it.

She wished she could let rip and tell him to take a hike and not give a damn. But the Brookes-Lyon children had been raised on a diet of diplomacy and were masters of the art of telling someone to go to hell in such a way that they immediately started planning the best route to get there. Well, Neil and Meredith were. She normally just stood there with a mouth full of teeth.

Jaci wrinkled her nose; some things never changed.

If she wasn't going to rip Mr. Rich-but-Creepy a new one—and she wasn't because she had the confrontational skills of a wet noodle—then she should remove herself, she decided.

"If you leave, I'll follow you."

Dear God, now he was reading her mind? "Please don't. I'm really not interested."

"But I haven't told you that I'm going to finance a film or that I own a castle in Germany, or that I own a former winner of the Kentucky Derby," he whined, and Jaci quickly suppressed her eye roll.

And I will never *tell you that my childhood home is a seventeenth-century manor that's been in my family for over four hundred years. That my mother is a third cousin to the queen and that I am, distantly, related to most of the royal families in Europe. They don't impress me, so you, with your pretentious attitude, haven't a chance.*

And, just a suggestion, use some of that money you

say you have to buy a decent suit, some shampoo and to get your teeth cleaned.

"Excuse me," Jaci murmured as she ducked around him and headed for the ballroom doors.

As she approached the elevators, congratulating herself on her getaway, she heard someone ordering an elderly couple to get out of the way and she winced as she recognized Toad's nasally voice. Glancing upward at the numbers above the elevator, she realized that if she waited for it he'd catch up to her and then she'd be caught in that steel box with him, up close and personal. There was no way he'd keep his hands or even—gack!—his tongue to himself. Thanks, but she'd rather lick a lamppost. Tucking her clutch bag under her arm, she glanced left and saw an emergency exit sign on a door and quickly changed direction. She'd run down the stairs; he surely wouldn't follow.

Stairs, lobby, taxi, home and a glass of wine in a bubble bath. Oh, yes, that sounded like heaven.

"My limousine is just outside the door."

The voice to her right made her yelp and she whirled around, slapping her hand to her chest. Those sludgy eyes looked feral, as if he were enjoying the thrill of the chase, and his disgusting soul patch jiggled as his wet lips pulled up into a smarmy smile. Dear God, he'd been right behind her and she hadn't even sensed him. Street smarts, she had none.

Jaci stepped to the side and looked past him to the empty reception area. Jeez, this was a nightmare... If she took the stairs she would be alone with him, ditto the elevators. Her only option was to go back to the ballroom where there were people. Across the room, the elevator doors opened on a discreet chime and Jaci watched as a tall man, hands in the pockets of his tuxedo pants, walked out toward the ballroom. Broad shoulders, trim waist, long legs. His dark hair was tapered, with the top styled into a tousled mess. He had bright, light eyes under dark brows and what she imagined was a three-day-old beard. She knew that profile, that face. Ryan?

Neil's Ryan? Jaci craned her neck for a better look.

God, it *was* the grown-up version—and an even more gorgeous version—of that young man she'd known so long ago. Hard, tough, sexy, powerful; a man in every sense of the word. Jaci felt her stomach roll over and her throat tighten as tiny flickers of electricity danced across her skin.

Instant lust, immediate attraction. And he hadn't even noticed her yet.

And she *really* needed him to notice her. She called out his name and he abruptly stopped and looked around.

"Limo, outside, waiting."

Jaci blinked at Mr. Toad and was amazed at his persistence. He simply wasn't going to give up until he got her into his car, into his apartment and naked. She'd rather have acid-coated twigs shoved up her nose. Seeing Ryan standing there, head cocked, she thought that there was maybe one more thing she could do to de-barnacle herself.

And, hopefully, Ryan wouldn't object.

"Ryan! Darling!"

Jaci stepped to her right and walked as fast as she possibly could across the Italian marble floor, and as she approached Ryan, she lifted her arms and wound them around his neck. She saw his eyes widen in surprise and felt his hands come to rest on her hips, but before he could speak, she slapped her mouth on his and hoped to dear Lord that he wouldn't push her away.

His lips were warm and firm beneath hers and she felt his fingers dig into her hips, their heat burning through the fabric of her dress to warm her skin. Her fingers touched the back of his neck, above the collar of his shirt, and she felt tension roll through his body.

Ryan yanked his head back and those penetrating eyes met hers, flashing with an emotion she couldn't identify. She expected him to push her away, to ask her what the hell she thought she was doing, but instead he yanked her closer and his mouth covered hers again. His tongue licked the seam between her lips and, without hesitation, she opened up, allowing him to taste her, to know her. A strong arm around her waist pulled her flush against him and then her breasts were flat against his chest, her stomach resting against his—*hello, Nelly!*—erection.

Their kiss might have lasted seconds, minutes, months or years, Jaci had no idea. When Ryan finally pulled his mouth away, strong arms still holding her against him, all she was capable of doing was resting her forehead on his collarbone while she tried to get her bearings. She felt as if she'd stepped away from reality, from time, from the ornate lobby in one of the most renowned hotels in the world and into another dimension. That had never happened to her before. She'd never been so swept away by passion that she felt as if she'd had an out-of-body experience. That it had happened with someone who was little more than a stranger totally threw her.

"Leroy, it's good to see you," Ryan said, somewhere above her head. Judging by his even voice, he was very used to being kissed by virtual strangers in fancy hotels. *Huh.*

"I was hoping that you would be here. I was on my way to find you," Ryan blithely continued.

"Ryan," Leroy replied.

Knowing she couldn't stay pressed against Ryan forever—sadly, because she felt as if she belonged there—Jaci lifted her head and tried to wiggle out of his grip. She was surprised when, instead of letting her go, he kept her plastered to his side.

"I see you've met my girl."

Jaci's head snapped back and she narrowed her eyes as she looked up into Ryan's urbane face. His girl?

His.

Girl?

Her mouth fell open. Bats-from-hell, he didn't remember her name! He had no idea who she was.

Mr. Toad pulled a thin cheroot from the inside pocket of his jacket and jammed it into the side of his mouth. He narrowed his eyes at Jaci. "You two together?"

Jaci knew that she often pulled on her Feisty Girl mask, but she'd never owned an invisibility cloak. Jaci opened her mouth to tell them to stop talking about her as if she wasn't there, but Ryan pinched her side and her mouth snapped shut. Mostly from indignant surprise. "She's my girlfriend. As you know, I've been out of town and I haven't seen her for a couple of weeks."

Weeks, years… Who was counting?

Leroy didn't look convinced. "I thought that she was leaving."

"We agreed to meet in the lobby," Ryan stated, his voice calm. He brushed his chin across the top of her head and Jaci shivered. "You obviously didn't get my message that I was on my way up, honey."

Honey? Yep, he definitely didn't have a clue who she

was. But the guy lied with calm efficiency and absolute conviction. "Let's go back inside." Ryan gestured to the ballroom.

Leroy shook his head. "I'm going to head out."

Thank God and all his angels and archangels for small mercies! Ryan, still not turning her loose, held out his right hand for Leroy to shake. "Nice to see you, Leroy, and I look forward to meeting with you soon to finalize our discussions. When can we get together?"

Leroy ignored his outstretched hand and gave Jaci another up-and-down look. "Oh, I'm having second thoughts about the project."

Project? What project? Why was Ryan doing business with Leroy? That was a bit of a silly question since she had no idea what business Ryan, or the amphib, was in. Jaci sent her brand-new boyfriend an uncertain glance. He looked as inscrutable as ever, but she sensed that beneath his calm facade, his temper was bubbling.

"I'm surprised to hear that. I thought it was a done deal," Ryan said, his tone almost bored.

Leroy's smile was nasty. "I'm not sure that I'm ready to hand that much money to a man I don't know all that well. I didn't even know you had a girlfriend."

"I didn't think that our *business* deal required that level of familiarity," Ryan responded.

"You're asking me to invest a lot of money. I want to be certain that you know what you are doing."

"I thought that my track record would reassure you that I do."

Jaci looked from one stubborn face to the other.

"The thing is… I have what you want so I suggest that if I say jump, you say how high."

Jaci sucked in breath, aghast. But Ryan, to his credit,

didn't dignify that ridiculous statement with a response. Jaci suspected that Leroy didn't have a clue that Ryan thought he was a maggot, that he was fighting the urge to either punch Leroy or walk away. She knew this because his fingers were squeezing her hand so hard that she'd lost all feeling in her digits.

"Come now, Ryan, let's not bicker. You're asking for a lot of money and I feel I need more reassurances. So I definitely want to spend some more time with you—" Leroy's eyes traveled up and down her body and Jaci felt as if she'd been licked by a lizard "—and with your lovely girlfriend, as well. And, in a more businesslike vein, I'd also like to meet some of your key people in your organization." Leroy rolled his cheroot from one side of his mouth to the other. "My people will call you."

Leroy walked toward the elevators and jabbed a finger on the down button. When the doors whispered open, he turned and sent them an oily smile.

"I look forward to seeing you both soon," he said before he disappeared inside the luxurious interior. When the doors closed, Jaci tugged her hand from Ryan's, noting his thunderous face as he watched the numbers change on the board above the elevator.

"Dammittohellandback," Ryan said, finally dropping her hand and running his through his short, stylishly messy hair. "The manipulative cretin."

Jaci took two steps backward and pushed her bangs out of her eye. "Look, seeing you again has been...well, odd, to say the least, but you do realize that I can't do this?"

"Be my girlfriend?"

"Yes."

Ryan nodded tersely. "Of course you can't, it would never work."

One of the reasons being that he'd then have to ask her who she was...

Besides, Ryan, as she'd heard from Neil, dated supermodels and actresses, singers and dancers. His old friend's little sister, neither actress-y nor supermodel-ly, wasn't his type, so she shrugged and tried to ignore her rising indignation. But, judging by the party in his pants while he was kissing her, maybe she was his type...just a little.

Ryan flicked her a cool look. "He's just annoyed that you rebuffed him. He'll forget about you and his demands in a day or two. I'll just tell him that we had a massive fight and that we split up."

Huh. He had it all figured out. Good for him.

"He's your connection, it's your deal, so whatever works for you," she said, her voice tart. "So...'bye."

Ryan shoved his hand through his hair. "It's been interesting. Why don't you give him ten minutes to leave then use the elevators around the corner? You'd then exit at the east doors."

She was being dismissed and she didn't like it. Especially when it was by a man who couldn't remember her name. Arrogant sod! Pride had her changing her mind. "Oh, I'm not quite ready to leave." She looked toward the ballroom. "I think I'll go back in."

Jaci saw surprise flicker in his gorgeous eyes. He wanted to get rid of her, she realized, maybe because he was embarrassed that he couldn't recall who she was. Not that he looked embarrassed. But still...

"Interesting seeing you *again*, Ryan," she said in a catch-a-clue voice.

A puzzled frown pulled his brows together. "Maybe we should have coffee, catch up."

Jaci shook her head and handed him a condescending smile. "*Honey*, you don't even know who I am so what, exactly, would be the point? Goodbye, Ryan."

"Okay, busted. So who are you?" Ryan roughly demanded. "I know that I know you..."

"You'll work it out," Jaci told him and heard him mutter a low curse as she walked away. But she wasn't sure if he would connect her with the long-ago teenager who'd hung on his every word. She doubted it. Her mask was intact and impenetrable. There was no hint of the insecure girl she used to be...on the outside, anyway. Besides, it would be fun to see his face when he realized that she was Neil's sister, the woman Neil, she assumed, wanted him to help navigate the "perils" of New York City.

Well, she was an adult and she didn't need her brother or Ryan or any other stupid man doing her any favors. She could, and would, navigate New York on her own.

And if she couldn't, her brother and his old friend would be the last people whom she'd allow to witness her failure.

"Then how about another kiss to jog my memory?" Ryan called out just as she was about to walk into the ballroom.

She turned around slowly and tipped her head to the side. "Let me think about that for a minute... Mmm...no."

But hot damn, Jaci thought as she walked off, she was tempted.

Two

Jaci slipped into the crowd and placed her fist into her sternum and tried to regulate her heart rate and her breathing. She felt as if she'd just experienced a wild gorge ride on a rickety swing and she was still trying to work out which way was up. She so wanted to kiss him again, to taste him again, to feel the way his lips moved over hers. He'd melted all her usual defenses and it felt as if he was kissing her, the *real* her. It was as if he'd reached inside her and grabbed her heart and squeezed...

That had to be a hormone-induced insanity because stuff like that didn't happen and especially not to her. She was letting her writer's imagination run away with her; this was real life, not a romantic comedy. Ryan was hot and sexy and tough, but that was what he looked like, wasn't what he was. *As you do, everybody wears masks to conceal who and what lies beneath*, she reminded herself. Sometimes what was concealed was harmless—she didn't think that her lack of confidence hurt anybody but herself—and occasionally people, including her ex-fiancé, concealed secrets that were devastating.

Clive and his secrets… Hadn't those blown up in their faces? It was a small consolation that Clive had fooled her clever family, too. They'd been so thrilled that, instead of the impoverished artists and musicians she normally brought home to meet her family, she'd snagged an intellectual, a success. A *politician*. In hindsight, she'd been so enamored by the attention she'd received by being Clive's girlfriend—not only from her family but from friends and acquaintances and the press—that she'd been prepared to put up with his controlling behavior, his lack of respect, his inattention. After years of being in the shadows, she'd loved the spotlight and the new sparky and sassy personality she'd developed to deal with the press attention she received. Sassy Jaci was the brave one; she was the one who'd moved to New York, who walked into crowded ballrooms, who planted her lips on the sexiest man in the room. Sassy Jaci was who she was going to be in New York, but this time she'd fly solo. No more men and definitely no more fading into the background…

Jaci turned as her name was called and she saw her friends standing next to a large ornamental tree. Relieved, she pushed past people to get to them. Her fellow script-writers greeted her warmly and Shona handed her a champagne glass. "Drink up, darling, you're way behind."

Jaci wrinkled her nose. "I don't like champagne." But she did like alcohol and it was exactly what she needed, so she took a healthy sip.

"Isn't champagne what all posh UK It girls drink?" Shona asked cheerfully and with such geniality that Jaci

immediately realized that there was no malice behind
her words.

"I'm not an It girl," Jaci protested.

"You were engaged to a rising star in politics, you attended the same social events with the Windsor boys, you
are from a very prominent British family."

Well, if you looked at it like that. Could she still be
classified as an It girl if she'd hated every second of said
socializing?

"You did an internet search on me," Jaci stated, resigned.

"Of course we did," Shona replied. "Your ex-fiancé
looks a bit like a horse."

Jaci giggled. Clive did look a bit equine.

"Did you know about his…ah…how do I put this?
Outside interests?" Shona demanded.

"No," Jaci answered, her tone clipped. She hadn't even
discussed Clive's extramural activities with her family—
they were determined to ignore the crotchless-panty-
wearing elephant in the room—so there was no way she
would dissect her ex–love life with strangers.

"How did you get the job?" Shona asked.

"My agent sold a script to Starfish over a year ago.
Six weeks ago Thom called and said that they wanted to
develop the story further and asked me to work on that,
and to collaborate on other projects. So I'm here, on a
six-month contract."

"And you write under the pen name of JC Brookes?
Is that because of the press attention you received?" Wes
asked.

"Partly." Jaci looked at the bubbles in her glass. It
was easier to write under a pen name when your parent,
writing under her *own* name, was regarded as one of the

most detailed and compelling writers of historical fiction in the world.

Wes smiled at her. "When we heard that we were getting another scriptwriter, we all thought you were a guy. Shona and I were looking forward to someone new to flirt with."

Jaci grinned at his teasing, relieved that the subject had moved on. "Sorry to disappoint." She placed her glass on a tall table next to her elbow. "So, tell me about Starfish. I know that Thom is a producer but that's about all I know. When is he due back? I'd actually like to meet the man who hired me."

"He and Jax—the big boss and owner—are here tonight, but they socialize with the movers and shakers. We're too far down the food chain for them," Shona cheerfully answered, snagging a tiny spring roll off a passing tray and popping it into her mouth.

Jaci frowned, confused. "Thom's not the owner?"

Wes shook his head. "Nah, he's Jax's second in command. Jax stays out of the spotlight but is very hands-on. Actors and directors like to work for him, but because they both have a low threshold for Hollywood drama, they are selective in whom they choose to work with."

"Chad Bradshaw being one of the actors they won't work with." Shona used her glass to gesture to a handsome older man walking past them.

Chad Bradshaw, legendary Hollywood actor. So that was why Ryan was here, Jaci thought. Chad had received an award earlier and it made sense that Ryan would be here to support his father. Like Chad, Ryan was tall and their eyes were the same; they could be either a light blue or gray, depending on his mood. Ryan might not remember her but she recalled in Technicolor detail the young man Neil had met at the London School of Economics. In between fantasizing about Ryan and writing stories with him as her hero inspiration, she'd watched the interaction between Ryan and her family. It had amused her that her academic parents and siblings had been fascinated by the fact that Ryan lived in Hollywood and that he was the younger brother of Ben Bradshaw, the young darling of Hollywood who was on his way to becoming a screen legend himself. Like the rest of the world, they'd all been shocked at Ben's death in a car accident, and his passing and funeral had garnered worldwide, and Brookes-Lyon, attention. But at the time they knew him, many years before Ben's death, it seemed as if Ryan was from another world, one far removed from the one the Brookes-Lyon clan occupied, and he'd been a breath of fresh air.

Ryan and Neil had been good friends and Ryan hadn't been intimidated by the cocky and cerebral Brookes-Lyon clan. He'd come to London to get a business degree, she remembered, and dimly recalled a dinner conversation with him saying something about wanting to get out of LA and doing something completely different from his father and brother. He visited Lyon House every couple of months for nearly a year but then he left the prestigious college. She hadn't seen him since. Until he kissed the hell out of her ten minutes ago.

Jaci pursed her lips in irritation and wondered how he kissed women whose names he *did* know. If he kissed them with only a smidgeon more skill than he had her, then the man was capable of melting polar ice caps.

He was *that* good and what was really, really bad was that she kept thinking that he had lips and that she had lips and that hers should be under his…*all the damn time*.

Phew. Problematic, Jaci thought.

* * *

Ryan "Jax" Jackson nursed his glass of whiskey and wished that he was in his apartment stretched out on his eight-foot-long couch and watching his favorite sports channel on the huge flat-screen that dominated one wall of his living room. He glanced at his watch, grateful to see that the night was nearly over. He'd had a run-in with Leroy, kissed the hell out of a sexy woman and now he was stuck in a ballroom kissing ass. He'd much rather be kissing the blonde's delectable ass... Dammit, who the hell was she? Ryan discarded the idea of flicking through his mental black book of past women. He knew that he hadn't kissed that mouth before. He would've remembered that heat, that spice, the make-him-crazy need to have her. So *who* was she?

He looked around the room in the hope of seeing her again and scowled when he couldn't locate her. Before the evening ended, he decided, he'd make the connection or he'd find her and demand some answers. He wouldn't sleep tonight if he didn't. He caught a flash of a blond head and felt his pants tighten. It wasn't her but if the thought of seeing her again had him springing up to half-mast, then he was in trouble. Trouble that he didn't need.

Time to do a mental switch, he decided, and deliberately changed the direction of his thoughts. What was Leroy's problem tonight? He'd agreed, in principle, to back the film and now he needed more assurances? *Why?* God, he was tired of the games the very rich boys played; his biggest dream was to find an investor who'd just hand over a boatload of money, no questions asked.

And that would be the day that gorgeous aliens abducted him to be a sex slave.

Still, he was relieved that Leroy had left; having his

difficult investor and his DNA donor in the room at the same time was enough to make his head explode. He hadn't seen Chad yet but knew that all he needed to do was find the prettiest woman in the room and he could guarantee that his father—or Leroy, if he were here—would be chatting her up. Neither could keep his, as Neil used to say, pecker in his pants despite having a wife at home.

What was the point of being married if you were a serial cheater? Ryan wondered for the millionth time.

Ryan felt an elbow in his ribs and turned to look into his best friend's open face. "Hey."

"Hey, you are looking grim. What's up?" Thom asked.

"Tired. Done with this day and this party," Ryan told him.

"And you're avoiding your father."

Well, yeah. "Where is the old man?"

Thom lifted his champagne glass to his right. "He's at your nine o'clock, talking to the sexy redhead. He cornered me and asked me to talk to you, to intercede on his behalf. He wants to *reconnect*. His word, not mine."

"So his incessant calls and emails over the past years have suggested," Ryan said, his expression turning cynical. "Except that I am not naive to believe that it's because he suddenly wants to play happy families. It's only because we have something he wants." As in a meaty part in their new movie.

"He would be great as Tompkins."

Ryan didn't give a rat's ass. "We don't always get what we want."

"He's your father," Thom said, evenly.

That was stretching the truth. Chad had been his guardian, his landlord and an absent presence in his life.

Ryan knew that he still resented the fact that he'd had to take responsibility for the child he created with his second or third or fifteenth mistress. To Chad, his mother's death when he was fourteen had been wildly inconvenient. He was already raising one son and didn't need the burden of another.

Not that Chad had ever been actively involved in his, or Ben's, life. Chad was always away on a shoot and he and Ben, with the help of a housekeeper, raised themselves. Ben, just sixteen months older than him, had seen him through those dark and dismal teenage years. He'd idolized Ben and Ben had welcomed him into his home and life with open arms. So close in age, they'd become best buds within weeks and he'd thought that there was nothing that could destroy their friendship, that they had each other's backs, that Ben was the one person who would never let him down.

Yeah, funny how wrong he could be.

Ben. God, he still got a lump in his throat just thinking about him. He probably always would. When it came to Ben he was a cocktail of emotions. Betrayal always accompanied the grief. Hurt, loss and anger also hung around whenever he thought of his best friend and brother. God, would it ever end?

The crowds in front of him parted and Ryan caught his breath. There she was… He'd kissed that wide mouth earlier, but between the kiss and dealing with Leroy he hadn't really had time to study the compact blonde. Short, layered hair, a peaches-and-cream complexion and eyes that fell somewhere between deep brown and black.

Those eyes… He knew those eyes, he thought, as a memory tugged. He frowned, immediately thinking of his time in London and the Brookes-Lyon family. Neil had mentioned in a quick email last week that his baby sister was moving to New York... What was her name again? Josie? Jackie... Close but still wrong... Jay-cee! Was that her? He narrowed his eyes, thinking it through. God, it had been nearly twelve years since he'd last seen her, and he struggled to remember the details of Neil's shy sibling. Her hair was the same white-blond color, but back then it hung in a long fall to her waist. Her body, now lean, had still been caught in that puppy-fat stage, but those eyes... He couldn't forget those eyes. Rich, deep brown, almost black Audrey Hepburn eyes, he thought. Then and now.

Jesus. He'd kissed his oldest friend's baby sister.

Ryan rubbed his forehead with his thumb and index finger. With everything else going on in his life, he'd completely forgotten that she was moving here and that Neil had asked him to make contact with her. He'd intended to once his schedule lightened but he never expected her to be at this post-awards function. And he certainly hadn't expected the shy teenager to have morphed into this stunningly beautiful, incredibly sexy woman; a woman who had his nerve endings buzzing. On the big screen in his head he could see them in their own private movie. She'd be naked and up against a wall, her legs around his waist and her head tipped back as he feasted on that soft spot where her neck and shoulders met...

Ryan blew out a breath. He was a movie producer, had dabbled in directing and he often envisioned scenes in his head, but never had one been so sexual, so sensual. And one starring his best and oldest friend's kid sister? That was just plain weird.

Sexy.

But still weird.

As if she could feel his eyes on her, Jaci turned her head and looked directly at him. The challenging lift of her eyebrow suggested that she'd realized that he'd connected the dots and that she was wondering what he intended to do about it.

Nothing, he decided, breaking their long, sexually charged stare. He was going to do jack about it because his sudden and very unwelcome attraction to Jaci was something he didn't have time to deal with, something he didn't *want* to deal with. His life was complicated enough without adding another level of crazy to it.

Frankly, he'd had enough crazy to last a lifetime.

Jaci stumbled through the doors to Starfish Films at five past nine the next morning, juggling her tote bag, her mobile, two scripts and a mega-latte, and decided that she couldn't function on less than three hours of sleep anymore. If someone looked up the definition of *cranky* in the dictionary, her picture next to the word would explain it all.

It hadn't helped that she'd spent most of the night reluctantly reliving that most excellent kiss, recalling the strength of that masculine, muscular body, the fresh, sexy smell of Ryan's skin. It had been a long time since she'd lost any sleep over a man—even during the worst of their troubles she'd never sacrificed any REMs for Clive—and she didn't like it. Ryan was sex on a side plate but she wasn't going to see him again. Ever. Besides, she hadn't relocated cities to dally with hot men, or any men. This job was what was important, the only thing that was important.

This was her opportunity to carve out a space for herself in the film industry, to find her little light to shine in. It might not be as bold or as bright as her mother's but it would be hers.

Frowning at the empty offices, she stepped up to her desk and dropped the scripts to the seat of her chair. This was the right choice to make, she told herself. She could've stayed in London; it was familiar and she knew how to tread water. Except that she felt the deep urge to swim…to do more and be more. She had been given an opportunity to change her life and, although she was soul-deep scared, she was going to run with it. She was going to prove, to herself and to her family, that she wasn't as rudderless, as directionless—as useless—as they thought she was.

This time, this job, was her one chance to try something different, something totally out of her comfort zone. This was her time, her life, her dream, and nothing would distract her from her goal of writing the best damn scripts she could.

Especially not a man with blue-gray eyes and a body that made her hormones hum.

Shona peeked into their office and jerked her head. "Not the best day to be late, sunshine. A meeting has started in the conference room and I suggest you get there."

"Meeting?" Jaci yelped. She was a writer. She didn't do meetings.

"The boss men are back and they want to touch base," Shona explained, tapping a rolled-up newspaper against her thigh. "Let's go."

A few minutes later, Shona pushed through the door at the top of the stairs and turned right down the identical hallway to the floor below. Corporate office buildings were all the same, Jaci thought, though she did like the framed movie posters from the 1940s and 1950s that broke up the relentless white walls.

Shona sighed and covered her mouth as she yawned. "We're all, including the boss men, a little tired and a lot hungover. Why we have to have a meeting first thing in the morning is beyond me. Jax should know better. Expect a lot of barking."

Jaci shrugged, not particularly perturbed. She'd lived with volatile people her entire life and had learned how to fly under the radar. Shona stopped in front of an open door, placed her hand between Jaci's shoulder blades and pushed her into the room. Jaci stumbled forward and knocked the arm of a man walking past. His coffee cup flew out of his hand toward his chest, and his cream dress shirt, sleeves rolled up past his elbows, bloomed with patches of espresso.

He dropped a couple of blue curses. "This is all I freakin' need."

Jaci froze to the floor as her eyes traveled up his coffee-soaked chest, past that stubborn, stubble-covered chin to that sensual mouth she'd kissed last night. She stopped at his scowling eyes, heavy brows pulled together. Oh, jeez...*no*.

Just no.

"Jaci?" Coffee droplets fell from his wrist and hand to the floor. "What the hell?"

"Jax, this is JC Brookes, our new scriptwriter," Thom said from across the room, his feet on the boardroom table and a cup of coffee resting on his flat stomach. "Jaci, Ryan 'Jax' Jackson."

He needed a box of aspirin, to clean up—the paper napkins Shona handed him weren't any match for a full cup of coffee—and to climb out of the rabbit hole he'd climbed into. He'd spent most of last night tossing and turning, thinking about that slim body under his hands, the scent of her light, refreshing perfume still in his nose, the dazzling heat and spice of her mouth.

He'd finally dozed off, irritated and frustrated, hours after he climbed into bed, and his few hours of sleep, starring a naked Jaci, hadn't been restful at all. As a result, he didn't feel as if he had the mental stamina to deal with the fact that the woman starring in his pornographic dreams last night was not only his friend's younger sister but also the screenwriter for his latest project.

Seriously? Why was life jerking his chain?

His mind working at warp speed, he flicked Jaci a narrowed-eyed look. "JC Brookes? You're him? Her?"

Jaci folded her arms across her chest and tapped one booted foot. How could she look so sexy in the city's uniform of basic black? Black turtleneck and black wide-leg pants… It would be boring as hell but she'd wrapped an aqua cotton scarf around her neck, and blue-shaded bracelets covered half her arm. He shouldn't be thinking about her clothes—or what they covered—right now, but he couldn't help himself. She looked, despite the shadows under those hypnotically brown eyes, as hot as hell. Simply fantastic. Ryan swallowed, remembering how feminine she felt in his arms, her warm, silky mouth, the way she melted into him.

Focus, Jackson.

"What the hell? You're a scriptwriter?" Ryan demanded, trying to make all the pieces of the puzzle fit. "I didn't know that you write!"

Jaci frowned. "Why should you? We haven't seen each other for twelve years."

"Neil didn't tell me." Ryan, still holding his head, kneaded his temples with his thumb and index finger. "He should've told me."

Now he sounded like a whining child. Freakin' perfect.

"He doesn't know about the scriptwriting," Jaci muttered, and Ryan, despite his fuzzy shock, heard the tinge of hurt in her voice. "I just told him and the rest of my family that I was relocating to New York for a bit."

Ryan pulled his sticky shirt off his chest and looked at Thom again. "And she got the job how?"

Thom sent him a what-the-hell look. "Her agent submitted her script, our freelance reader read it, then Wes, then me, then you read the script. We all liked it but you fell in love with it! Light coming on yet?"

Ryan looked toward the window, unable to refute Thom's words. He'd loved Jaci's script, had read it over and over, feeling that tingle of excitement every time. It was an action comedy but one with heart; it felt familiar and fresh, funny and emotional.

And Jaci, his old friend's little sister, the woman he'd kissed the hell out of last night, was—thanks to fate screwing with him—the creator of his latest, and most expensive, project to date.

And his biggest and only investor, Leroy Banks, had hit on her and now thought that she was his girlfriend.

Oh, and just for kicks and giggles, he really wanted to do her six ways to Sunday.

"Could this situation be any more messed up?" Ryan grabbed the back of the closest chair and dropped his head, ignoring the puddles of coffee on the floor. He groaned aloud. Banks thought that his pseudo girlfriend was the hottest thing on two legs. Ryan understood why. He also thought she was as sexy as hell.

She was also now the girlfriend he couldn't break up with because she was his damned scriptwriter, one of—how had Banks put it?—his key people!

"I have no idea why you are foaming at the mouth, dude," Thom complained, dropping his feet to the floor. He shrugged. "You and Jaci knew each other way back when, so what? She was employed by us on her merits, with none of us knowing of her connection to you. End of story. So can we just get on with this damn meeting so that I can go back to my office and get horizontal on my couch?"

"Uh...no, I suggest you wait until after I've dropped the next bombshell." Shona tossed the open newspaper onto the boardroom table and it slid across the polished top. As it passed, Ryan slapped his hand on it to stop its flight. His heart stumbled, stopped, and when it resumed its beat was erratic.

In bold color and filling half the page was a picture taken last night in the reception area outside the ballroom of the Forrester-Graham. One of his hands cradled a bright blond head, the other palmed a very excellent butt. Jaci's arms were tight around his neck, her mouth was under his, and her long lashes were smudges on her cheek.

The headline screamed Passion for Award-Winning Producer!

Someone had snapped them? When? And why hadn't he noticed? Ryan moved his hand to read the small amount of text below the picture.

Ryan Jackson, award-winning producer of *Stand Alone*—the sci-fi box office hit that is enthralling audiences across the country—celebrates

in the arms of JC Brookes at the Television and
Film Awards after-party last night. JC Brookes is
a scriptwriter employed by Starfish Films and is
very well-known in England as the younger daugh-
ter of Fleet Street editor Archie Brookes-Lyon and
his multi-award-winning author wife, Priscilla. She
recently broke off her longstanding engagement to
Clive Egglestone, projected to be a future prime
minister of England, after he was implicated in a
series of sexual scandals.

What engagement? What sexual scandals? More news
that his ever-neglectful friend had failed to share. Jaci
had been engaged to a politician? Ryan just couldn't see
it. But that wasn't important now.

Ryan pushed the newspaper down the table to Thom.
When his friend lifted his eyes to meet his again, his
worry and horror were reflected in Thom's expression.
"Well, hell," he said.

Ryan looked around the room at the nosy faces of
his most trusted staff before pulling a chair away from
the table and dropping into it. It wasn't in his nature to
explain himself but this one time he supposed, very reluctantly, that it was necessary. "Jaci and I know each
other. She's an old friend's younger sister. We are not in
a relationship."

"Doesn't explain the kiss," Thom laconically stated.

"Jaci, on impulse, kissed me because Leroy was hitting on her and she needed an escape plan."

That explained her first kiss. It certainly didn't explain why he went back for a second, and hotter, taste.
But neither Thom nor his staff needed to know that little
piece of information. *Ever*.

"I told him that she was my girlfriend and that we hadn't seen each other for a while." Ryan kept his attention on Thom. "I had it all planned. When next we met and if Leroy asked about her, I was going to tell him that we'd had a fight and that she'd packed her bags and returned to the UK. I did not consider the possibility that my five-minute girlfriend would also be my new scriptwriter."

Thom shrugged. "This isn't a big deal. Tell him that you fought and that she left. How is he going to know?"

Ryan pulled in a deep breath. "Oh, maybe because he told me, last night, that he wants to meet the key staff involved in the project, and that includes the damned scriptwriter."

Thom groaned. "Oh, God."

"Not sure how much help he is going to be." Ryan turned around and looked at a rather bewildered Jaci, who had yet to move away from the door. "My office. Now."

Well, hell, he thought as he marched down the hallway to his office. It seemed that his morning could, after all, slide further downhill than he'd expected.

Three

Jaci waited in the doorway to Ryan's office, unsure whether she should step into his chaotic space—desks and chairs were covered in folders, scripts and stacks of papers—or whether she should she just stay where she was. He was in his private bathroom and she could hear a tap running and, more worrying, the steady stream of inventive cursing.

Okay, crazy, crazy morning and she had no idea what had just happened. It felt as if everyone in that office had been speaking in subtext and that she was the only one who did not know the language. All she knew for sure was that Jax was Ryan and Ryan was Neil's friend—and her new boss—and that he was superpissed.

And judging by their collective horror, she also knew that Banks's clumsy pass and her kissing Ryan had consequences bigger than she'd imagined.

Ryan walked out of the bathroom, shirtless and holding another dress shirt, pale green this time, in his right hand. He was coffee-free and that torso, Jaci thought on an appreciative, silent sigh, could grace the cover of any male fitness magazine. His shoulders were broad and strongly muscled as were his biceps and his pecs. And that stomach, sinuously ridged, was a work of art. Jaci felt that low buzz in her stomach, the tingling spreading across her skin, and wondered why it had taken her nearly twenty-eight years to feel true attraction, pure lust. Ryan Jackson just had to breathe to make her quiver...

"You used to be Ryan Bradshaw. Why Jackson?" Jaci blurted. It was all she could think of to say apart from "Kiss me like you did last night." Since she was already in trouble, she decided to utter the only other thought she had to break the tense, sexually saturated silence.

Ryan blinked, frowned and then shook his shirt out, pulling the fabric over one arm. "You heard that Chad was my father, that Ben was my brother, and you assumed that I used the same surname. I don't," Ryan said in a cool voice.

She stepped inside and shut the door. "Why not?"

"I met Chad for the first time when I was fourteen, when the court appointed me to live with him after my mother's death. He dumped my mother two seconds after she told him she was pregnant and her name appeared on my birth certificate. I'd just lost her, and I wasn't about to lose her name, as well." Ryan machine-gunned his words and Jaci tried to keep up.

Ryan rubbed his hand over his face. "God, what does that have to do with anything? Moving rapidly on..."

Pity, Jaci thought. She would've liked to hear more about his childhood, about his relationship with his famous brother and father, which was, judging by his pain-filled and frustrated eyes, not a happy story.

"Getting back to the here and now, how the hell am I going to fix this?" Ryan demanded, and Jaci wasn't sure whether he was asking the question of her or himself.

"Look, I'm really sorry that I caused trouble for you by kissing you. It was an impulsive action to get away from Frog Man."

Ryan shoved his other arm into his sleeve and pulled the edges of his shirt together, found the buttons and their corresponding holes without dropping his eyes from her face.

"He was persistent. And slimy. And he wouldn't take the hint!" Jaci continued. "I'm sorry that the kiss was captured on camera. I know what an invasion of your privacy that can be."

Ryan glanced at the paper that he'd dropped onto his desk. "You seem to know what you're talking about." Ryan tipped his head. "Sexual scandals? Engaged?"

"All that and more." Jaci tossed her head in defiance and held his eyes. "You can find it all online if you want some spicy bedtime reading."

"I don't read trash."

"Well, I'm not going to tell you what happened," Jaci stated, her tone not encouraging any argument.

"Did I ask you to?"

Hell, he hadn't, Jaci realized, as a red tide crept up her neck. *Jeez, catch a clue. The guy kissed you. That doesn't mean he's interested in your history.*

Time to retreat. What had they been talking about? Ah, their kiss. "Look, if you need me to apologize to your girlfriend or wife, then I will." She thought about adding

"I won't even tell her that you initiated the second kiss" but decided not to fan the flames.

"I'm not involved with anyone, which is about the only silver lining there is."

Jaci pushed her long bangs to one side. "Then I really don't understand what the drama is all about. We're both single, we kissed. Yeah, it landed up in the papers, but who cares?"

"Banks does and I told him that you're my girlfriend."

Jaci lifted her hands in confusion. This still wasn't any clearer. "So?"

Ryan started to roll up his sleeves, his expression devoid of all emotion. But his eyes were now a blistering blue, radiating frustration and a healthy dose of anxiety. "In order to produce *Blown Away*, to get the story you conceived and wrote onto the big screen, to do it justice, I need a budget of a hundred and seventy million dollars. I don't like taking on investors, I prefer to work solo, but the one hundred million I have is tied up at the moment. Besides, with such a big budget, I'd also prefer to risk someone else's money and not my own. Right now, Banks is the only thing that decides whether *Blown Away* sees the light of day or gets skipped over for a smaller-budget film.

"I thought that we were on the point of signing the damn contract but now he just wants to jerk my chain," Ryan continued.

"But why?"

"Because he knows that I caught him hitting on my girlfriend and he's embarrassed. He wants to remind me who's in control."

Okay, now she got it, but she wished she hadn't. She'd

put a hundred-million deal in jeopardy? With a kiss? When she messed up, she did a spectacular job of it.

Jaci groaned. "And I'm your screenwriter." She shoved her fingers into her hair. "One of the project's key people."

"Yep." Ryan sat down on the edge of his desk and picked up a glass paperweight and tossed it from hand to hand. "We can't tell him that you only threw yourself into my arms because you found him repulsive… If you do that, we'll definitely wave goodbye to the money."

"Why can't I just stay in the background?" Jaci asked. She didn't want to—it wasn't what she'd come to the city to do—but she would if it meant getting the film produced. "He doesn't know that I wrote the script."

Ryan carefully replaced the paperweight, folded his arms and gave her a hard stare. After a long, charged minute he shook his head. "That's problematic for me. Firstly, you did write that script and you should take the credit for it. Secondly, I don't like any forms of lying. It always comes back to bite me on the ass."

Wow, an honest guy. She thought that the species was long extinct.

Jaci dropped into the nearest chair, sat on top of a pile of scripts, placed her elbows on her knees and rested her chin in the palm of her hand. "So what do we do?"

"I need you as a scriptwriter and I need him to fund the movie, so we do the only thing we can."

"Which is?"

"We become what Leroy and the world thinks we are, a couple. Until I have the money in the bank, and then we can quietly split, citing irreconcilable differences."

Jaci shook her head. She didn't think she could do it. She'd just come out of a relationship, and she didn't think she could be in another one, fake or not. She was determined to fly solo. "Uh…no, that's not going to work for me."

"You got me into this situation by throwing yourself into my arms, and you're going to damn well help me get out of it," Ryan growled.

"Seriously, Ryan—"

Ryan narrowed his eyes. "If I recall, your contract hasn't be signed…"

It took twenty seconds for his words to sink in. "Are you saying that you won't formalize my contract if I don't do this?"

"I've already bought the rights for the script. It's mine to do what I want with it. I did want some changes and I would prefer it if you write those, but I could ask Wes, or Shona, to do it."

"You're blackmailing me!" Jaci shouted, instantly infuriated. She glanced at the paperweight on his desk and wondered if she could grab it and launch it toward his head. He might not lie but he wasn't above using manipulation, the dipstick!

Ryan sighed and placed the paperweight on top of a pile of folders. "Look, you started all this trouble, and you need to figure out how to end it. Consider it as part of your job description."

"Don't blame this on me!"

Ryan lifted an eyebrow in disbelief and Jaci scowled. "At least not all of it! The first kiss was supposed to be a peck, but you turned it into a hot-as-hell kiss!" Jaci shouted, her hands gripping the arms of the chair.

"What the hell was I supposed to do? You plastered yourself against me and slapped your mouth on mine!" Ryan responded with as much, maybe even more, heat.

"Do you routinely shove your tongue into a stranger's mouth?"

"I knew that I'd met you, dammit!" Ryan roared. He sprang to his feet and stormed over to his window and stared down at the tiny matchbox cars on the street below. Jaci watched as he pulled in a couple of deep breaths, amazed that she was able to fight with this man, shout at him, yet she felt nothing but exhilaration. No feelings of inadequacy or guilt or failure.

That was new. Maybe New York, with or without this crazy situation, was going to be good for her.

"So what are we going to do?" Jaci asked after a little while. It was obvious that they had to do something because walking away from her dream job was not an option. She was not going to go back to London without giving this opportunity her very best shot. Giving up now was simply not an option. She had to prove herself and she'd do it here in New York City, the toughest place around. Nobody would doubt her then.

"Do you want to see this film produced? Do you want to see your name in the credits?" Ryan asked without turning around.

Well, duh. "Of course I do," she softly replied. This was her big break, her opportunity to be noticed, to get more than her foot through the door. She'd been treading water for so long, she couldn't miss this opportunity to ride the wave to the beach.

"Then I need Banks's money."

"Is he the only investor around? Surely not."

"Firstly, they don't grow on trees. I've also spent nearly eighteen months thrashing out the agreement. I can't waste any more time on him and I can't let that effort be for nothing."

There was no way out of this. "And to get his money we have to become a couple."

"A fake couple," Ryan hastily corrected her. "I don't want or need a real relationship."

Jeez, chill. She didn't want a relationship, either.

"So I can see some garden parties in the Hamptons in our future. Maybe theater or opera tickets, dinners at upscale restaurants because Banks will want to show me how important he is and he'll want to show you what you missed out on."

"Oh, joy."

Ryan shoved his hands in his hair and tugged. "We don't have a choice here and we have to make this count."

Jaci rubbed her hands over her face. Who would've thought that an impulsive kiss could lead to such a tangle? She didn't have a choice but to go along with Ryan's plan, to be his temporary girlfriend. If she didn't, months of work—Ryan's, hers, Thom's—would evaporate, and she doubted that Ryan and Thom would consider working with her again if she was the one responsible for ruining their deal with Banks.

She slumped in her chair. "Okay, then. It's not like we—I—have much of a choice anyway."

Ryan turned and gripped the sill behind him, his broad back to the window. He sighed and rubbed his temple with the tips of his fingers, his action telling her that he had a headache on board. Lucky she hadn't clobbered him with that paperweight; his headache would now be a migraine.

"For all we know, Leroy might change his mind about socializing and we'll be off the hook," Ryan said, rolling his head from side to side.

"What do you think are the chances of that happening?" Jaci asked.

"Not good. He doesn't like the fact that I have you. He'll make me jump through hoops."

"Because you're everything he isn't," Jaci murmured.

"What do you mean?"

You're tall, hot and sexy. Charming when you want to be. You're successful, an acclaimed producer and businessman. You're respected. Leroy, as far as she knew, just had oily hair and enough money to keep a third-world economy buoyant. Jaci stared at her hands. She couldn't tell Ryan any of that; she had no intention of complimenting her blackmailer. Even if he could kiss to world-class standards.

"Don't worry about it." Jaci waved her words away and prayed that he wouldn't pursue the topic.

Thankfully he didn't. Instead he reached for the bottle of water on his desk and took a long sip. "So, as soon as I hear from Banks I'll let you know."

"Fine." Jaci pushed herself to her feet, wishing she could go back to bed and pull the covers over her head for a week or two.

"Jaci?"

Jaci lifted her eyes off her boots to his. "Yes?"

"We'll keep it completely professional at work. You're the employee and I'm the boss," Ryan stated. That would make complete sense except for the sexual tension, as bright and hot as a lightning arc, zapping between them. Judging by his hard tone and inscrutable face, Ryan was ignoring that sexual storm in the room. She supposed it would be a good idea if she did the same.

Except that her feet were urging her to get closer to

him, her lips needed to feel his again, her... God, this
was madness.

"Fine. I'll just get back to work then?"

"Yeah. I think that would be a very good idea."

When Jaci finally left his office, Ryan dropped into
his leather chair and rolled his head from side to side,
trying to release the tension in his neck and shoulders.
In the space of ten hours, he'd acquired a girlfriend and
the biggest deal of his life was placed in jeopardy if he
and Jaci didn't manage to pull off their romance. He
hadn't been exaggerating when he told Jaci that Leroy
would be furious if he realized that Jaci was just using
him as an excuse to put some distance between her and
his wandering hands...but hell, talk about being in the
wrong place at the wrong time!

It was the kiss—that fantastic, hot, sexy meeting
of their mouths—that caused the complications. And,
dammit, she was right. The first kiss, initiated by her,
had been tentative and lightweight and he was the one
who'd taken it deeper, hotter, wetter. Oh, she hadn't protested and had quickly joined him on the ride. A ride he
wouldn't mind taking to its logical conclusion.

Concentrate, moron. Sex should have been low on his
priority list. It wasn't but it should have been.

When he'd come back down to earth and seen Banks's
petulant face—pouty mouth and narrowed eyes—he'd
realized that he'd made a grave miscalculation. Then he'd
added fuel to the fire when he'd informed him that Jaci
was his girlfriend. Banks wanted Jaci and didn't like the
fact that Ryan had her, and because of that, Ryan would
be put through a wringer to get access to Banks's cash.

Like his father, Banks was the original playground

bully; he instantly wanted what he couldn't and didn't have. Ryan understood that, as attractive as he found Jaci—and he did think that she was incredibly sexy—for Leroy his pursuit of her had little to do with Jaci but, as she'd hinted at earlier, everything to do with him. With the fact that she was with him, that he had her…along with a six-two frame, a reasonable body and an okay face.

This was about wielding power, playing games, and what should've been a tedious, long but relatively simple process would now take a few more weeks and a lot more effort. He knew Leroy's type—his father's type. He was a man who very infrequently heard the word *no*, and when he did, he didn't much care for it. In the best-case scenario, they'd go on a couple of dinners and hopefully Leroy would be distracted by another gorgeous woman and transfer his attention to her.

The worst-case scenario would be Leroy digging his heels in, stringing him along and then saying no to funding the movie. Ryan banged his head against the back of his chair, feeling the thump of the headache move to the back of his skull.

The thought that his father had access to the money he needed jumped into his brain.

Except that he'd rather drill a screwdriver into his skull than ask Chad for anything. In one of his many recent emails he'd skimmed over, his father had told him that he, and some cronies, had up to two hundred million to invest in any of his films if there was a part in one of his movies for him. It seemed that Chad had conveniently forgotten that their final fight, the one that had decimated their fragile relationship, had been about the industry, about money, about a part in a film.

After Ben's death, his legions of friends and his fans,

wanting to honor his memory, had taken to social media
and the press to "encourage" him—as a then-indie film-
maker and Ben's adoring younger brother—to produce a
documentary on Ben's life. Profits from the film could
be donated to a charity in Ben's name. It would be a fit-
ting memorial. The idea snowballed and soon he was
inundated with requests to do the film, complete with
suggestions that his father narrate the nonexistent script.

He'd lost the two people he'd loved best in that accident, the same two people who'd betrayed him in
the worst way possible. While he tried to deal with his
grief—and anger and shock—the idea of a documentary
gained traction and he found himself being swept into
the project, unenthusiastic but unable to say no without explaining why he'd rather swim with great whites
in chum-speckled water. So he'd agreed. One of Ben's
friends produced a script he could live with and his father agreed to narrate the film, but at the last minute
Chad told him that he wanted a fee for lending his voice
to the documentary.

And it hadn't been a small fee. Chad had wanted ten
million dollars and, at the time, Ryan, as the producer,
hadn't had the money. Chad—Hollywood's worst father
of the year—refused to do it without a financial reward,
and in doing so he'd scuttled the project. He was relieved
at being off the hook, felt betrayed by Ben, heartbroken
over Kelly, but he was rabidly angry that Chad, their
father, had tried to capitalize on his son's death. Their
argument was vicious and ferocious and he'd torn into
Chad as he'd wanted to do for years.

Too much had been said, and after that blowout he
realized how truly alone he really was. After a while
he started to like the freedom his solitary state afforded

him and really, it was just easier and safer to be alone. He liked his busy, busy life. He had the occasional affair and never dated a woman for more than six weeks at a time. He had friends, good friends he enjoyed, but he kept his own counsel. He worked and he made excellent films. He had a good, busy, productive life. And if he sometimes yearned for more—a partner, a family— he ruthlessly stomped on those rogue thoughts. He was perfectly content.

Or he would be if he didn't suddenly have a fake girlfriend who made him rock-hard by just breathing, a manipulative investor and a father who wouldn't give up.

Four

Jaci, sitting cross-legged on her couch, cursed when she heard the insistent chime telling her that she had a visitor. She glanced at her watch. At twenty past nine it was a bit late for social visits. She was subletting this swanky, furnished apartment and few people had the address, so whoever was downstairs probably had the wrong apartment number.

She frowned and padded over to her front door and pressed the button. "Yes?"

"It's Ryan."

Ryan? Of all the people she expected to be at her door at twenty past nine—she squinted at her watch, no, that was twenty past ten!—Ryan Jackson was not on the list. Since leaving his office four days before, she hadn't exchanged a word with him and she'd hoped that his ridiculous idea of her acting as his girlfriend had evaporated.

"Can I come up?" Ryan's terse question interrupted her musings.

Jaci looked down at her fuzzy kangaroo slippers—a gag Christmas gift from her best friend, Bella—and winced. Her yoga pants had a rip in the knee and her sweatshirt was two sizes too big, as it was one of Clive's that she'd forgotten to return. Her hair was probably spiky from pushing her fingers into it and she'd washed off her makeup when she'd showered after her run through Central Park after work.

"Can this wait until the morning? It's late and I'm dressed for bed."

She knew it was ridiculous but she couldn't help hoping that Ryan would assume that she was wearing a sexy negligee and not clothes a bag lady would think twice about.

"Jaci, I don't care what you're wearing so open the damn door. We need to talk."

That sounded ominous. And Ryan sounded determined enough, and arrogant enough, to keep leaning on her doorbell if he thought that was what it would take to get her to open up. Besides, she needed to hear what he had to say, didn't she?

But, dammit, the main reason why her finger hit the button to open the lobby door was because she wanted to see him. She wanted to hear his deep, growly voice, inhale his cedar scent—deodorant or cologne? Did it matter?—have an opportunity to ogle that very fine body.

Jaci placed her forehead on her door and tried to regulate her heart rate. Having Ryan in her space, being alone with him, was dangerous. This apartment wasn't big—this was Manhattan, after all—and her bedroom was a hop, skip and a jump away from where she was standing right now.

You cannot possibly be thinking about taking your boss to bed, Jacqueline! Seriously! Slap some sense into yourself immediately!

Ryan's sharp knock on the door had her jerking her head back. Because her father had made her promise that she wouldn't open the door without checking first—apparently the London she'd lived in for the past eight years was free of robbers and rapists—she peered through the peephole before flipping the lock and the dead bolt on the door.

And there he was, dressed in a pair of faded jeans and a long-sleeved, collarless black T-shirt. He held a leather jacket by his thumb over his shoulder and, with the strips of black under his eyes and his three-day beard, he looked tired but tough.

Ryan leaned his shoulder into the door frame and kept his eyes on her face, which Jaci appreciated. "Hey."

Soooo sexy. "Hello. What are you doing here? It's pretty late," she said, hoping that he missed the wobble in her voice.

"Leroy Banks finally returned my call. Can I come in?"

Jaci nodded and stepped back so that he could walk into the room. Ryan immediately dropped his jacket onto the back of a bucket chair and looked around the room, taking in the minimalist furniture and the abstract art. "Not exactly Lyon House," he commented.

"Nothing is," Jaci agreed. Her childhood home was old and stately but her parents had made it a home. It had never been a showpiece; it was filled with antiques and paintings passed down through the generations but also packed with books and dog leashes, coffee cups and magazines.

"Did your mother ever get that broken stair fixed? I remember her nagging your father to get it repaired. She said it had been driving her mad for twenty years."

Did she hear longing in his voice or was that her imagination? Ryan had always been hard to read, and her ability to see behind the inscrutable mask he wore had not improved with age. And she was too tired to even try. "Nope, the stair is still cracked. It will never be fixed. She just likes to tease my father about his lack of handyman skills. Do you want something to drink? Coffee? Tea? Wine?"

"Black coffee would be great. Black coffee with a shot of whiskey would be even better."

She could do that. Jaci suggested that Ryan take a seat but instead he followed her to the tiny galley kitchen, his frame blocking the doorway. "So, how are you enjoying work?"

Jaci flashed him a quick smile at his unexpected question. "I'm loving it. I'm working on the romcom at the moment. You said that you want changes done to *Blown Away* but I need to spend some time with you and Thom to find out exactly what you want and, according to your PA, your schedules are booked solid."

"I'll try to carve out some time for you soon, I promise."

Jaci went up onto her toes to reach the bottle of whiskey on the top shelf. Then Ryan's body was flush up against hers, his chest to her back, and with his extra height he easily took the bottle off the shelf. Jaci expected him to immediately move away but she felt his nose in her hair, felt the brush of his fingers on her hip.

She waited with bated breath to see if he'd turn her to face him, wondered whether he'd place those broad hands on her breasts, lower that amazing mouth to hers...

"Here you go."

The snap of the whiskey bottle hitting the counter jerked her out of her reverie, and then the warmth of his body disappeared. With a dry mouth and a shaking hand, Jaci unscrewed the cap to the bottle and dumped a healthy amount of whiskey into their cups.

Hoo, boy! And down, girl!

"It's a hell of a coincidence that you, the sister of my old friend, had a script accepted by me, by us," Ryan said, lifting his arms up so that he gripped the top of the door frame. The action made his T-shirt ride up, showing a strip of tanned, muscled abdomen and a hint of fabulous oblique muscles. Jaci had to bite her tongue to stop her whimper.

"Actually, I'm not at all surprised that you like the script. After all, *Blown Away* was your idea."

"Mine?" Ryan looked confused.

Jaci poured hot coffee into the cups and picked them up. She couldn't breathe in the small kitchen—too much distracting testosterone—and she needed some space between her and this sexy man. "Shall we sit?"

Ryan took his cup, walked back to the living room and slumped into the corner of her couch. Jaci took the single chair opposite him and immediately put her feet up onto the metal-and-glass coffee table.

Ryan took a sip of his coffee and raised his eyebrows. "Explain."

Jaci blew air across the hot liquid before answering him. "You came down to Lyon House shortly before you dropped out of uni—"

"I didn't drop out, I graduated."

Jaci shook her head. "But you're the same age as Neil and he was in his first year."

Ryan shrugged, looking uncomfortable. "Accelerated classes. School was easy."

"Lucky you," Jaci murmured. Unlike her siblings, she'd needed to work a lot harder to be accepted into university, which she'd flunked out of halfway through her second year. She thought that she and Ryan had that in common, but it turned out that he was an intellectual like her sister. And brother. And her parents. She was, yet again, the least cerebral person in the room.

Lucky she'd had a lot of practice at being that.

"So, the script?" Ryan prompted.

"Oh! Well, you came home with Neil and the two of you were playing chess. It was raining cats and dogs. I was reading." Well, she'd been watching him, mooning over him, but he didn't need to know that! Ever. "You were talking about your careers and Neil asked you if you were going into the movie business like your father."

Jaci looked down into her cup. "You said that your dad and Ben had that covered, that you wanted your own light to shine in." His words had resonated with her because she understood them so well. She'd wanted exactly the same thing. "You also said that you were going to go into business management and that you were going to stay very far away from the film industry."

"As you can see, that worked out well," Ryan said, his comment bone-dry and deeply sarcastic.

"Neil said that you were fooling yourself, that it was as much in your blood as it was theirs." Jaci quirked an eyebrow. "He called that one correctly."

"Your brother is a smart man."

As if she'd never noticed.

"Anyway, Neil started to goad you. He tossed out plots and they were all dreadful. You thought his ideas were ridiculous and started plotting your own movie about a burnt-out cop and his feisty female newbie partner who were trying to stop a computer-hacking serial bomber from taking a megacity hostage. I was writing, even then, mostly romances but I took some of the ideas you tossed out, wrote them down and filed them. About eighteen months ago I found that file and the idea called to me, so I sat down and wrote the script." Jaci sipped her coffee. "I'm not surprised that you liked the script but I am surprised that you own a production company and that I'm now working for you."

Ryan's eyes pinned her to her chair. "Me, too." He pushed his hand through his hair. "Talking of non-scriptwriting work—"

Jaci sighed. "Toad of Toad Hall—"

"—has issued his first demand." Jaci groaned but Ryan ignored her. "He's invited us to join him at the premiere of the New York City Ballet Company's new production of *Swan Lake*."

Jaci groaned again but more loudly and dramatically this time.

"You don't like ballet? I thought all girls like ballet," he said, puzzled. "And didn't your family have season tickets to the Royal Opera House to watch both ballet and opera?"

"They did. They dragged me along to torture me." Jaci pulled a face. "I much prefer a rock concert to either."

"But you'll do it?"

Jaci wrinkled her nose. "I suppose I have to. When is it?"

"Tomorrow evening. Black tie for me, which means a ball gown, or something similar, for you." His eyes focused on the rip in her pants before he lifted amused eyes to hers. "Think you can manage that?"

Jaci looked horrified. "You're kidding me right? Tomorrow?"

"Evening. I'll pick you up at six."

Jaci leaned back in her chair and placed her arm over her eyes. "I don't have anything to wear. That one cocktail dress I brought over was it."

Ryan took a sip from his cup and shrugged. "Last time I checked, there are about a million clothes stores in Manhattan."

She'd made a promise to herself that, now that she was free of Clive and free of having her outfits picked apart by the fashion police in the tabloids, she could go back to wearing clothes that made her feel happy, more like herself. Less staid, more edgy. When she left London with the least offensive of the clothes that had been carefully selected by the stylist Clive employed to shop for her, she'd promised herself that she would overhaul her wardrobe. She'd find the vintage shops and the cutting-edge designers and she would wear clothes that were a little avant-garde, more edgy. And she wouldn't wear another ball gown unless someone put a gun to her head.

Unfortunately, risking so many millions wasn't a gun, it was a freaking cannon…

She'd thought she was done with playing it safe.

"You're still frowning," Ryan said. "This is not a big deal, Jaci. How difficult can shopping be?"

"Only a man would say that," Jaci replied, bouncing to her feet. She slapped her hands onto her hips and jerked her head. "What do you want me to wear?"

Ryan shrugged and looked confused. "Why the hell should I care?"

"It's your party, Ryan, your deal. Give me a clue... regal, flamboyant, supersexy?"

"What the hell are you talking about?" Ryan demanded. "Put a dress on, show up, smile. That's it. Just haul something out of your closet and wear it. You must have something you can wear."

He really didn't get it. "Come with me," she ordered.

Ryan, still holding his coffee, followed her down the supershort hallway to the main bedroom. Jaci stomped over to the walk-in closet and flung the doors open. She stepped inside and gestured to the mostly empty room. Except for the umber cocktail dress she'd worn the other night, nearly every single item hanging off the rod and on the shelves was a shade of black.

Ryan lifted an eyebrow. "Do you belong to a coven or something? Or did the boring stuff get left behind when they robbed you?"

"I have enough clothes to stock my own store," Jaci told him with frost in her voice. "Unfortunately they aren't on this continent."

Ryan looked at her empty shelves again. "I can see that. Why not?"

Jaci pushed her hair behind her ears. "They are in storage, as I wasn't intending to wear them anymore."

"I can't believe that I am having a conversation about clothes but...and again...why not?"

Jaci stared at the floor and folded her arms across her chest. After a long silence, Ryan put his finger under her chin and lifted her eyes to his. "Why not, Jace?"

"I only brought a few outfits with me to the city. I was going to trawl the vintage shops and edgy boutiques to find clothes that were me…clothes that I liked, that I wanted to wear, clothes that made me feel happy. Now I have to buy a staid and boring ball gown that I'll probably never wear again."

Ryan narrowed his eyes. "Why does it have to be staid and boring?"

"You're in the public eye, Ryan. And there's a lot riding on this deal," Jaci pointed out. "It's important that I look the part."

The corners of Ryan's mouth twitched. "If our deal rests on what you are wearing then I'm in bigger trouble than I thought. You're making too big a deal of this, Jace. Wear whatever the hell you want, wherever and whenever. Trust me, I'm more interested in what's under the clothes anyway."

He really wasn't taking this seriously. "Ryan, impressions matter."

"Maybe if you're a politician who has a stick up his ass," Ryan retorted, looking impatient.

He didn't understand; he hadn't been crucified in the press for, among other things, his clothes. He hadn't been found wanting. She'd had enough of that in the United Kingdom. She didn't want to experience it on two continents. That was why she was trying to stay out of the public eye, why she was avoiding functions exactly like the one Ryan was dragging her to. And if she had to go, and it seemed as if she had little choice in the matter, she'd wear something that didn't attract attention, that would let her fly under the radar.

She waved her hand in the air in an attempt to dismiss the subject. "I'll sort something out."

Ryan sent her a hot look. "I don't trust you… You'll

probably end up buying something black and boring. Something safe."

Well, yes. That was the plan.

Ryan put his hands on his hips. "You want vintage and edgy?"

Where was he going with this? "For my day-to-day wardrobe, yes."

"And for the ball gown?" Jaci's shrug was his answer. "I'm taking you shopping," Ryan told her with a stubborn look on his face.

Ryan...shopping? With her? For a ball gown? Jaci couldn't picture it. "I don't think... I'm not sure."

"You need a dress, and I am going to get you into one that isn't suitable for a corpse," Ryan promised her, his face a mask of determination. "Tomorrow."

"It would be a lot easier if you just excused me from the ballet," Jaci pointed out.

"Not going to happen," Ryan said as his eyes flicked from her face to the bed and back again. And, just like that, her insecurities about her clothes—okay, about herself— faded away, replaced by hot, flaming lust. She saw his eyes deepen and darken and she knew what he was thinking because, well, she was thinking it, too. How would it feel to be on that bed together, naked, limbs tangled, mouths fused, creating that exquisite friction that was older than time?

"Jaci?"

"Mmm?" Jaci blinked, trying to get her eyes to focus. When they did she saw the passion blazing in Ryan's eyes. If that wasn't a big enough clue as to what he wanted to do then there was also the impressive ridge in his pants. "The only real interest I have in your clothes is how to get you out of them. I really want to peel off that ridiculous shirt and those ratty pants to see what you're wearing underneath."

Nothing—she wasn't wearing a damn thing. Jaci touched the top of her lip with her tongue and Ryan groaned.

"I'm desperate to do what we're both thinking," Ryan said, his voice even huskier coated with lust. "But that would complicate this already crazy situation. It would be better if I just left."

Better for whom? Not for her aching, demanding libido, that was for sure. Jaci was glad that she didn't utter those words out loud. She just stood there as Ryan brushed past her. At the entrance of her room, he stopped and turned to look back at her. "There's a coffee shop around the corner from here. Laney's?"

"Yes."

"I'll meet you there at nine to go shopping."

Jaci nodded. "Okay."

Ryan's smile was slow and oh so sexy. "And, Jace? I value authenticity above conventionality. Just an FYI."

Ryan left the coffee shop holding two takeout cups and looked right and then left, not seeing Jaci anywhere. The outside tables were full and he brushed past some suits to stand in a patch of spring sunshine, lifting his leg behind him to place his foot against the wall.

He had a million things to do this morning but he was taking a woman shopping. There was something very wrong with this picture. He had a couple of rules when it came to the women he dated: he never slept over, he never took the relationship past six weeks, and he never did anything that could, even vaguely, be interpreted as something a "couple" would do. Clothes shopping was right up there at the top of the list.

A hundred million dollars…

Yeah, that was a load of bull. Jaci could turn up in nipple caps and a thong and it wouldn't faze him. He didn't care jack about what Leroy, or people in general, thought. Yet Jaci seemed to be determined to hit the right note, sartorially speaking. Something about their conversation last night touched Ryan in a place that he thought was long buried. He couldn't believe that the sexy, stylish, so outwardly confident Jaci could be so insecure about what she wore and how she looked. Somebody had danced in her head, telling her that she wasn't enough exactly as she was, and that made him as mad as hell.

Maybe because it pushed a very big button of his own: the fact that, in his father's eyes, he'd never been or ever would be the son he wanted, needed, the son he lost. It was strange that he'd shared a little of his dysfunctional family life with Jaci; he'd never divulged any of his past before, mostly because it was embarrassing to recount exactly how screwed up he really was. That's what happened when you met your father and half brother for the first time at fourteen and within a day of you moving in, your father left for a six-month shoot across the country. He and Ben were left to work out how they were related, and they soon realized that they could either ignore each other—the house was cavernous enough that they could do that—or they could be friends and keep each other company. That need for company turned into what he thought was an unbreakable bond.

Ryan stared at the pavement and watched as a candy wrapper danced across the sidewalk, thinking that bonds could be broken. He had the emotional scars to prove it.

All it took was two deaths in a car crash and the subsequent revelation of an affair.

"Hi."

The voice at his elbow came out of nowhere and the cups in his hands rattled. God, he'd been so deep in thought that she'd managed to sneak up on him, something that rarely happened. Ryan looked into her face, noticed the splash of freckles across her nose that her makeup failed to hide and handed her a cup of coffee. Today she was wearing a pair of tight, fitted suit pants and a short black jacket. Too much black, Ryan thought. Too structured, too rigid.

But very New York.

"Thanks." Jaci sipped her coffee and lifted her face to the sun. "It's such a gorgeous day. I'd like to take my laptop and go to the park, find a tree and bang out a couple of scenes." She handed him a puppy-dog look. "Wouldn't you rather have me do that instead of shopping?"

"Nice try, but no go."

Ryan placed his hand on her lower back and steered her away from the wall. He could feel the warmth of her skin through the light jacket, and the curve of her bottom was just inches away. He was so damn tempted. Screw writing and shopping. His idea of how to spend a nice spring morning was to take this woman to bed.

Boss/employee, fake relationship/Leroy Banks, friend's kid sister…there were a bunch of reasons why that wasn't a viable option. But, hellfire, he really wanted to.

Ryan lifted his fingers to his mouth and let out a shrill whistle. Seconds later a taxi pulled up next to them. Ryan opened the door and gestured Jaci inside.

"Where to?"

Ryan started to give the address of his apartment then

mentally slapped himself and told the driver to take them to Lafayette Street in Soho. "If we don't find what we're looking for there, we'll head to Nolita."

He saw Jaci's frown. "Nolita?"

"North of little Italy," Ryan explained. "It's like a cousin to Soho. It also has curb-to-curb boutiques."

Her frown deepened. "I thought we were heading for Fifth Avenue and the department stores or designer stores there."

"Let's try something different," Ryan replied, eyeing her tailored jacket. The unrelenting black was giving him a headache. The plump, happy teenager he knew had loved bright colors, and he'd love to see her in those shades again. He operated in a fake world and if he had to be saddled with a girlfriend, pretend or not, then he wanted the real Jaci next to him, not the cardboard version of whom she thought she should be.

As he'd said, authenticity was a seldom-found commodity, and he wasn't sure why it was so important that he get it from her.

Ryan watched as the taxi driver maneuvered the car through the busy traffic. He was going shopping. With his fake girlfriend. Whom he wanted, desperately, to see naked.

All because a narcissistic billionaire also had the hots for her. Yes, indeed. There was something very wrong with this picture.

Five

Her previous visits to New York had always been quick ones and because of that, Jaci had never taken in the time to let the nuances of the city register. She'd visited Soho before but she'd forgotten about the elegant cast-iron architecture, the cobblestone streets, the colorful buildings and the distinct artistic vibe.

Obviously, the artists peddling their creations contributed to the ambience but she could also smell the art in the air, see it in the fabulous window displays, in the clothes of the people walking the streets. Jaci—for the first time in years—felt like the fish out of water. The old Jaci, the one she'd been before Clive and the stylist he insisted she used, dressed in battered jeans, Docs and her favorite Blondie T-shirt belonged in Soho. This Jaci in her funeral suit? Not so much.

Ryan, with his messy hair and his stubble and stunning eyes, would fit in anywhere. He wore a black-and-white plaid shirt under a black sweater, sleeves pushed up. His khaki pants and black sneakers completed his casual ensemble and he looked urban and classy. Hot.

Ryan paid the taxi driver and placed his hand on her back. He'd done that earlier and it was terrifying to admit how much she liked the gesture. His broad hand spanned the width of her back and it felt perfect, right there, just above the swell of her bottom.

Ryan gestured to the nearest boutique and Jaci sighed. Minimalistic, slick and, judging by the single black halter neck in the window, boring. But, she reluctantly admitted, it would probably be eminently suitable for an evening spent at the ballet.

Jaci followed Ryan to the shop window and he pulled the door open for her to enter. As she was about to step inside, he grabbed her arm to hold her back. "Hey, this isn't a torture session, Jace. If this isn't your type of place, then let's not waste our time."

Jaci sucked in her bottom lip. "It's the type of shop that Gail, my stylist, would take me to."

"But not your type of shop," Ryan insisted.

"Not my type of shop. Not my type of clothes. Well, not anymore," Jaci reluctantly admitted. "But I should just look around. The dress is for the ballet and I will be going with a famous producer and a billionaire."

Ryan let go of the door and pulled her back onto the pavement. He lifted his hand and brushed the arch of his thumb along her cheekbone. "I have a radical idea, Jaci. Why don't you buy something that you want to wear instead of wearing something you think you should wear?"

God, she wished she could. The thing was, her style was too rock-chick and too casual, as she explained to

Ryan. "Tight Nirvana T-shirts didn't project the correct image for a politician's SO."

"Jerk." Ryan dropped his eyes to her breasts, lingered and slowly lifted them again. Jaci's breath hitched at the heat she saw in the pale blue gray. Then his sexy mouth twitched. "There is nothing wrong, in my opinion, with a tight T-shirt." Jaci couldn't help her smile. "The thing is…you're not his fiancée anymore and you're not in London anymore. You can be anyone you want to be, dress how you wish. And that includes any function we attend as a fake couple."

He made it sound so simple… She wished it was that easy. Although she'd made up her mind to go back to dressing as she wanted to, old habits were hard to break. And sometimes Sassy Jaci wasn't as strong as she needed her to be. She still had an innate desire to please, to do what was expected of her, to act—and dress—accordingly. When she dressed and acted appropriately, her family approved. When she didn't they retreated and she felt dismissed. She was outgrowing her need for parental and sibling approval, but sometimes she simply wished that she was wired the same as them, that she could relate to them and they to her. But she was the scarlet goat in a family of sleek black sheep.

"Hey." Ryan tipped her chin up with his thumb and made her meet his startling eyes. "Come on back to me."

"Sorry."

"Just find something that you want to wear tonight. And if I think it's unsuitable then I'll tell you, okay?"

Jaci felt a kick of excitement, the first she'd felt about clothes and shopping for a long, long time. It didn't even come close to the galloping of her heart every time she laid eyes on Ryan, but it was still there.

Jaci reached up and curled her hand around his wrist, her eyes bouncing between his mouth and those long lashed eyes. She wanted to kiss him again, wanted to feel those clever lips on her, taste him. She wanted to—

Then he did as she'd mentally begged and kissed her. God, that mouth, those lips, that strong hand on her face. Kissing him in the sunlight on a street in Soho... Perfection. Jaci placed her hands on his waist and cocked her head to change the angle and Ryan, hearing her silent request, took the kiss deeper, sliding his tongue into her mouth to tangle with hers. Slow, sweet, sexy. He tasted of coffee and mint, smelled of cedar and soap. Jaci couldn't help the step that took her into his body, flush against that long, muscled form that welcomed her. She didn't care that they were in the flow of the pedestrian traffic, that people had to duck around them. She didn't hear the sniggers, the comments, the laughter.

There was just her and Ryan, kissing on a city street in the spring sunshine.

Jaci lost all perception of time; she had no idea how long it had been when Ryan pulled back.

Don't say it, Jaci silently begged. *Please don't say you're sorry or that it was a mistake. Just don't. I couldn't bear it.*

Ryan must have seen something on her face, must have, somehow, heard her silent plea, because he stepped away and jammed his hands into his pockets.

"I really need to stop doing that," he muttered.

Why? She rather liked it.

"We need to find you a dress," he said, in that sexy growl.

Jaci nodded and, wishing that she had the guts to tell him that she'd far prefer that he find them a bed, fell into step beside him.

* * *

They left another shop empty-handed and Jaci walked straight to a bench and collapsed onto it. Her feet were on fire, she was parched and was craving a cheeseburger. They'd visited more than ten shops and Ryan wouldn't let her buy any of the many dresses she'd tried on, and Jaci was past frustrated and on her way to irritated. "I'm sick of this. I need a vodka latte with sedative sprinkles."

Ryan sat on the bench next to her, and his cough sounded suspiciously like "lightweight." Jaci narrowed her eyes at him. "I would never have taken you for a shopaholic, Jackson."

"For the record, normally you couldn't get me to do this without a gun to my head."

Because there was a hundred million on the line…

"You're the one who is drawing this out," Jaci pointed out. "The second shop we visited had that black sheath that was imminently suitable. You wouldn't let me buy it."

"You hated it." Ryan wore an expression that Jaci was coming to realize was his stubborn face. "As I said, tonight I'd like you to wear something you feel sexy in."

I'd feel sexy wearing you… Moving the hell on.

"Denim shorts, a Ramones tee and cowboy boots?" Jaci joked, but she couldn't disguise the hopeful note in her voice.

His mouth quirked up in a sexy smile that set her hormones to their buzz setting. "Not tonight but I'd like to see that combination sometime."

Jaci crossed one leg over the other and twisted her body so that she was half facing him. Sick of discussing clothes, she changed the subject to something she'd been wondering about. "When did you open Starfish and why?"

Ryan took a long time to answer and when he started to speak, Jaci thought that he would tell her to mind her own business. "Neil was right, I couldn't stay away from the industry. I landed a job as business manager at a studio and I loathed it. I kept poking my nose into places it didn't belong, production, scripts, art, even direction. After I'd driven everybody mad, the owner took me aside and suggested I open up my own company. So I did." Ryan tipped his face up to the sun. "That was about six months before Ben died."

His dark designer shades covered his eyes, but she didn't need to see them to know that, on some level, he still mourned his brother. That he always would. "I'm so sorry about Ben, Ryan."

"Yeah. Thanks."

Jaci sucked in some air and asked the questions she, and a good portion of the world, still wondered about. "Why did they crash, Ryan? What really happened?"

Ryan shrugged. "According to the toxicology screen, he wasn't stoned or drunk—not that night, anyway. He wasn't suicidal, as far as we knew. Witnesses said that he wasn't driving fast. There was no reason why his Porsche left the road and plunged down that cliff. It was ruled a freak accident."

"I'm sorry." The words sounded so small, so weak. She bit her bottom lip. "And the woman who died along with him? Had you met her? Did you know her?"

"Kelly? Yeah, I knew her," Ryan replied, his voice harsh as he glanced at his watch. Subject closed, his face and body language stated. "It's nearly lunchtime. Want to hit a few more shops? If we don't find anything, we'll go back for that black sheath."

"Let's go back for that black sheath now," Jaci said

as she stood up, pulling her bag over her shoulder. As they stepped away from the bench, she saw a young woman holding four or five dresses on a hanger, her arm stretched above her head to keep the fabrics from skimming the ground. The top dress, under its plastic cover, made her heart stumble. It was a striking, A-line floor-length dress in watermelon pink with a deep, plunging, halfway-to-her-navel neckline.

Without hesitation she crossed the pavement and tapped the young woman on her shoulder. "Hi, sorry to startle you." She gestured to the garments. "I love these. Are they your designs?"

The woman nodded. "They are part of a consignment for The Gypsy's Caravan."

Jaci reached out and touched the plastic covering the top dress. It was simple but devastatingly so, edgy but feminine. It was a rock-chick dress trying to behave, and she was in love. The corners of Ryan's mouth kicked up when she looked at him.

"What do you think?" she asked, not quite able to release the plastic covering of the dress, her dress.

"I think that you love it." Ryan flashed his sexy smile at the woman carrying the dresses and Jaci was sure that she saw her knees wobble. This didn't surprise her in the least. Her knees were always jelly-like around Ryan.

"It looks like we're going where you are," Ryan said as he reached for the dresses and took them from her grasp, then held them with one hand so that they flowed down his back. With his height they didn't even come close to the dirty sidewalk. He placed his other hand on Jaci's back.

Jaci shook her head, planting her feet. "I don't think

it's suitable. It's too sexy… I mean, I couldn't wear a bra with it!"

After looking at her chest, Ryan lifted his eyebrows. "You don't need a bra." He grabbed her hand and tugged it. "It's the first time I've seen you remotely excited about a dress all morning. You're trying it on. Let's go."

"The black sheath is more appropriate."

"The black sheath is as boring as hell," Ryan whipped back. "Jace, I'm tired and sick of this. Let's just get this done, okay?"

Well, when he put it like that… He was still—despite their hot kisses and the attraction that they were trying, and failing, to ignore—the boss.

As an excuse, it worked for her.

In the end it was just the three of them who attended the ballet, and despite the fact that Ryan did his best to keep himself between her and Leroy, Jaci knew that he couldn't be her buffer all evening and at some point she would have to deal with Leroy on her own. The time, Jaci thought as she sent Ryan's departing back an anxious look, had come. It was intermission and Ryan, along with what seemed to be the rest of the audience, was making his way toward the bar for the twelve-year-old whiskey Leroy declared that he couldn't, for one more minute, live without.

Keeping as much distance as she could from him in the crowded, overperfumed space, she fixed her eyes on Ryan's tall frame, trying to keep her genial smile in place. It faltered when a busty redhead bumped her from behind and made her wobble on her too-high heels. She gritted her teeth when she felt Leroy's clammy grip on her elbow. *Ick*. Jaci ruthlessly held back her shiver of distaste as she pulled her arm from his grasp. Strange that Ryan, with one look, could heat her up from the inside out, that he could have her shivering in anticipation from a brief scrape of his hand against any part of her, yet Leroy had exactly the opposite effect. They were two ends of the attraction spectrum and she was having a difficult time hiding her reactions, good and bad, to both of them.

One because there was a hundred million on the line; the other because she was, temporarily, done with men and a dalliance with Ryan—her boss!—would not be a smart move. She wouldn't jeopardize her career for some hot sex…as wonderful as she knew that hot sex would be. Mmm, not that she'd ever had any hot sex, but a girl could dream. She'd had hurried sex and boring sex and blah sex but nothing that would melt her panties. Judging by the two kisses they'd shared, Ryan had a PhD in melting underwear.

Yep, just the thought had the thin cord of her thong warming; if she carried on with this train of thought she'd be a hot mess. Jaci straightened her back and mentally shook herself off. She was enough of a mess as it was. She was in New York to get a handle on her crazy life, to establish her career and to find herself. She was not supposed to be looking for ways to make it more complicated!

"I have a private investigator."

Jaci tucked her clutch bag under her arm and linked her fingers together. *Be polite, friendly but distant.* She could make conversation for ten minutes or so; she wasn't a complete social idiot. A private investigator? Why would he be telling her that? "Okay. Um…what do you use him for?"

"Background checks on business associates, employees," Leroy explained. His eyes were flat and cold and Jaci felt the hair on her arms rise. "When I was considering whether to go into business with Jackson, I had him investigated."

"He wouldn't have found anything that might have given you second thoughts," Jaci quickly replied.

Leroy cocked his head. "You seem very sure of that."

"Ryan has an enormous amount of integrity. He says what he means and means what he says." Jaci heard the heat in her voice and wished that she could dial it down. Leroy hadn't said anything to warrant her defense of Ryan but something in his tone, in his body language, had her fists up and wanting to box. This was very unlike her. She wasn't a fighter.

"Strange that you should be so sure of that since you've only known him for a few weeks," Leroy replied, his words silky. Leroy ran a small, pale hand down the satin lapels of his suit in a rhythmic motion. Where was he going with this? Jaci, deciding that silence was a good option, just held his reptilian eyes.

"So tell me, Jacqueline, how involved can you be with Ryan after knowing him for just seventeen days?"

"I broke up with my ex six weeks before that and sometimes love—" she tried not to choke on the word "—happens in unexpected places and at unexpected times." Jaci allowed herself a tiny, albeit cold, smile. "You really should hire better people, Leroy, because your PI's skills are shoddy. I've known Ryan for over twelve years. He attended university with my brother, and he was a guest in my parents' home. We've been in contact for far longer than two weeks." Jaci tacked on the last lie with minimal effort.

It was time for Sassy Jaci, she thought. She needed to throw politeness out the window, so she nailed Leroy with a piercing look. "Why the interest in me? And if you have to color outside the lines, there are hundreds of gorgeous, unattached girls, interested girls, out there you can dally with."

"My pursuit of you annoys Ryan and that puts him off guard. I like him off guard. But I do find you attractive and taking you from Ryan would be an added bonus." After a minute, he finally spoke again. "I like to have control in a relationship, whether that's business or personal."

That made complete sense, Jaci thought. "And Ryan won't be controlled."

"He will if he wants my money." Leroy's smile was as malicious as a snakebite. He lifted his hand and the tip of his index finger touched her bare shoulder and drifted down the inside of her arm. "He'll toe the line. They always do. Everyone has their price."

"I don't. Neither does Ryan."

"Everyone does. You just don't know what it is yet and neither do I."

There was a relentless determination in his eyes that made her think he was being deadly serious.

"This conversation has become far too intense," Leroy calmly stated. "You do intrigue me… You're very different from what I am used to, from the women I usually meet."

"Because I'm not rich, or plastic, or crazy?" Jaci demanded.

Leroy's laugh sounded like sandpaper on glass and it was as creepy as his smile. "At first, perhaps. But mostly you fascinate me because Ryan is fascinated by you. I want to know why."

There was that one-upmanship again, Jaci thought.

What was with this guy and his need to feel superior to Ryan? The chip on his shoulder was the size of a redwood tree. Didn't he realize that few men could compete with Ryan? Ryan was a natural leader, utterly and completely masculine, and one of his most attractive traits was the fact that he didn't care what people thought about him.

Leroy had a better chance of corralling the wind than he did of controlling Ryan. Why couldn't he see that? Couldn't he see Ryan was never going to kowtow to him, that he would never buckle?

Ryan marched to the beat of his own drum.

"Everything okay here?"

Jaci whirled around at Ryan's voice and reached for the glass of wine she'd ordered. Taking a big sip, she looked at him over her glass, her expression confused and uneasy.

"Everything is fine," Leroy said.

Ryan ignored him and kept his eyes on Jaci's face. "Jace?"

Jaci drank in his strong, steady presence and nodded. He held her stare for a while longer and eventually his expression cleared. He finally handed over Leroy's glass into his waiting hand, accompanied by a hard stare. Ryan wasn't a fool. He knew that words had been exchanged and Jaci knew that he'd demand to know what they'd discussed. How serious was Leroy's need to control Ryan? Jaci wasn't as smart about these things as her siblings were, but with her career and Ryan's film on the line, she couldn't afford to shove her head in the sand and play ostrich.

The lights flickered and Ryan placed his hand on her lower back. "Time to head back in," he said.

As Ryan led her back to their seats, Jaci thought that

they had to manage the situation and, right now, she was the only pawn on the chessboard. If she removed herself, Ryan and Leroy wouldn't have anything to tussle over. But they couldn't admit to their lie about being a couple; that would have disastrous consequences. But what if they upped the stakes, what if they showed Leroy that she was, in no uncertain terms, off-limits forever? Right now, as Ryan's girlfriend, there was room for doubt… Maybe they should remove all doubt.

Not giving herself time to talk herself out of the crazy idea that popped into her head, she stopped to allow an older couple to walk into the theater in front of her and slipped her hand into Ryan's, resting her head on his shoulder. She sent Leroy a cool smile. "There is one other thing your PI didn't dig up, Leroy."

Ryan's body tensed. "PI? What PI?"

Jaci ignored him and kept her eyes on Leroy's face. She watched as his eyebrows lifted, those eyes narrowed in focus. "And what might that be?"

Here goes, Jaci thought. *In for a penny and all that, upping the stakes, throwing the curveball.* "He wouldn't know that Ryan and I are deeply in love and that we are talking about marriage." She tossed Ryan an arch look. "I expect to be engaged really soon and I can't wait to wear Ryan's ring."

Six

What.
   The.
     Hell?

Two hours and a couple of lukewarm congratulations from Leroy later, and Ryan was still reeling from Jaci's surprise announcement and "what the hell" or other variations of the theme kept bouncing around his head. Leaving the theater, back teeth grinding, he guided Jaci through the door, his hand on her back. She'd, once again and without discussion, flipped his world on its head. *Thinking about marriage?* Did she *ever* think before she acted?

On the sidewalk, Ryan saw a scruffy guy approaching them from his right, an expensive camera held loosely in his hands, and he groaned. He immediately recognized Jet Simons. He was one of the most relentless—and annoying—tabloid reporters on the circuit. Part journalist, part paparazzo, all sleaze. Ryan knew this because the guy practically stalked him in the month following Ben's death. Jet had witnessed his grief and every day Ryan would pray that Jet wouldn't capture his anger at Ben and his pain at being betrayed by his brother and Kelly. He definitely hadn't wanted Jet to capture how alone he felt, how isolated. Soul-sucking bottom-feeder.

Ryan sent a back-the-hell-off look in his direction, which, naturally, Simons ignored. Dammit, he needed him around as much he needed a punch in the kidneys. Ryan grabbed Jaci's hand, hoping to walk away before they were peppered with questions.

"Leroy Banks and Jax Jackson," Simons drawled, stepping up to them and lifting his camera, the flash searing their eyes. "How's it hanging, guys?"

"Get out of my face or I'm going to shove that camera where it hurts," Ryan growled, pushing the lens away. Unlike the actors he worked with who played a cat-and-mouse game with the press, he didn't need to make nice with the rats.

The flash went off another few times and Ryan growled. He was about to make good on his threat when Simons lowered the camera and looked over it to give Jaci a tip-to-toe look, his gaze frankly appreciative. Ryan felt another snarl rumble in his throat and reminded himself that Jaci was his pretend girlfriend and that he had no right to feel possessive over her. The acid in his stomach still threatened to eat a hole through its lining.

Just punch him, caveman Ryan said from his shoulder, *you'll feel so much better after.*

Yeah, but sitting in jail on assault charges would suck.

"So, you're Jaci Brookes-Lyon," Simons said, his eyes appreciative. "Not Jax's usual type, I'll grant you that."

Ryan squeezed Jaci's hand in a silent reminder not to respond. It was good advice, and he should listen to it, especially since he still wanted to shove that lens down Simons's throat or up his…

"Mr. Banks, how you doing? You still in bed with Jackson? Figuratively speaking, that is? Where's Mrs. Banks?" Simons machine-gunned his words. "What do you think about Jax's little sweetie here? Do you think she is another six-weeker or does she have the potential to be more?"

Ryan heard Jaci's squawk of outrage but his attention was on Leroy's face, and his slow smile made Ryan's balls pull up into his body. Dammit, he was going to dump them right in it. He knew it as he knew his own signature. Ryan's mind raced, desperate for a subject change, but before he could even try to turn the conversation Leroy spoke again. "They are talking about marriage, so maybe I suspect she does—" he waited a beat before speaking again "—have potential, that is."

Ryan let fly with a creative curse and shook his head when he realized that his outburst just added a level of authenticity to Banks's statement. He knew that a vein was threatening to pop in his neck and he released a clenched fist. Maybe he should just punch Leroy, as well, and make his jail stay worth his while.

"So you're engaged?" Simons demanded, his face alight with curiosity.

"Look, that's not exactly…" Jaci tried to explain but Ryan tightened his grip on her hand and she muttered a low "Ow."

"Stop talking," Ryan ordered in her ear before turning back to Simons and pinning him to the floor with a hard glance. "Get the hell out of my face."

Simons must have realized that he was dancing on his last nerve because he immediately took a step backward and lifted his hands in a submissive gesture. *Wuss*, Ryan internally scoffed as he watched him walk away. When Simons was out of earshot, Ryan finally settled his attention on Banks and allowed him to see how pissed he was with him, too. "I don't know what game you're playing, Banks, but it stops right now."

Leroy shrugged. "I am the one financing your film so you don't get to talk to me like that."

Wusses. He was surrounded by them tonight.

"I haven't seen any of your money so you're not in any position to demand a damn thing from me," Ryan said, keeping his voice ice cold. Cold anger, he realized a long time ago, was so much more effective than ranting and raving. "And even if we do still do business together, it'll always be my movie. You will never call the shots. Think about that and come back to me if you think those are terms you can live with."

Banks flushed under Ryan's hard stare and Ryan thought that it was a perfect time to throw in one last threat. "And this thing you have for my girlfriend stops right here. Leave her the hell alone."

"Ryan…" Jaci tried to speak as he pulled her toward a taxi sitting behind Leroy's limo and yanked the door open. He bundled her inside and when she was seated, he gripped the sides of the door and glared at her. This was all her and her big mouth's fault! What the hell had she been thinking by telling Leroy that they were talking about marriage? And how could he still be so intensely angry with her but still want to rip her clothes off? How could he want to strangle and kiss her at the same time?

He was seriously messed up. Had been since this crazy woman dropped back into his life.

"Not one damn word," he ordered before slamming the door closed and walking around the back of the cab. He slid inside and Jaci opened her mouth again.

"Ryan, I need you to understand why—"

God, she seriously wasn't listening. "What part of 'not one damn word' didn't you understand?" he growled after he tossed the address to her place to the driver up front.

"I understand that you are angry—"

"Shut. Up." Ryan felt as if a million spiders were dancing under his skin and that his temper was bubbling, looking for a way to escape. He'd spent his teenage years with a volatile father who didn't give a damn about him, and when he did pay him some attention, it was always negative. He'd learned to ignore the disparaging comments, to show no reaction and definitely no emotion. His father had fed off drama, had enjoyed baiting him, so he'd learned not to lose control, but tonight he was damn close. Engaged? Him? The man who, thanks to his brother and Kelly, rarely dated beyond six weeks? Who would believe it? And he was engaged to Jaci, who wasn't exactly his type…mostly because she wasn't like the biddable, eager-to-please women he normally dated. God, he hadn't even slept with Jaci yet and he was half-way to being hitched? On what planet in what freaking galaxy was that fair?

"I need to explain. Leroy—"

Okay, obviously she had no intention of keeping quiet, and he had two options left to him. To strip sixteen layers of skin off her or to shut her up in the only way he knew how. Deciding to opt for the second choice, he twisted, leaned over and slapped his mouth on hers. He dimly heard her yelp of surprise, and taking advantage of her open mouth, he slid his tongue inside...

His world flipped over again as he licked into her mouth, his tongue sliding over hers. She tasted of mint and champagne and heated surprise. The scent of her perfume, something light but fresh, enveloped him and his hands tightened on her hips, his fingers digging into the fabric of the dress he'd helped her choose, the dress he so desperately wanted to whip off her to discover what lay underneath. The backs of his fingers skimmed the side of her torso, bumped up and over her ribs, across the swelling of her breasts. He wanted to cup her, to feel her nipple pucker into his hand, but he was damned if he'd give the taxi driver a free show. Knowing her, discovering her, could wait until later. He needed to delay gratification, even if his erection felt as if it was being strangled by his pants. He could do it but that didn't mean he had to like it.

He wanted her. He wanted all of her...

Jaci yanked him back to the present by whipping her mouth off his and pushing herself into the corner of the cab, as far away from him as possible. "What are you doing?"

That was obvious, wasn't it? "Kissing you."

Dark eyes flashed her annoyance. "You tell me to shut up and then you kiss me? Are you crazy?"

That was highly possible.

"You wouldn't shut up," Ryan pointed out, his temper reigniting as he remembered her stupid declaration.

"You wouldn't let me explain," Jaci retorted.

"Yeah, I can't wait to see what you come up with." Ryan retreated to his corner of the cab, knowing that a muscle was jumping in his cheek. "Why would you make up such a crazy story? Are you that desperate to be engaged, to show the world that someone wants to marry you, that you would just go off half-cocked? I don't want to be engaged. God, I've been battling to wrap my head around having a fake girlfriend, and now I have a fake fiancée? And that it's you? Jesus!"

Ryan would never have believed it possible if he didn't witness her already brown-black eyes darken to coals. Anger and pride flashed but he couldn't miss the hurt, couldn't help but realize that he'd pushed one button too many, that he'd gone too far. He fumbled for words as she turned away to stare out the window, her hands in a death grip in her lap.

But God, his work was *his life* and she was screwing with it. He wanted that hundred million, he wanted to share the risk with an investor. And the one he'd had on his hook he'd just cut loose because of this woman and her way of speaking without thinking, of screwing up his life.

And it killed him to know that if she made one move to sleep with him, even kiss him, he'd be all over her like a rash. He was a reasonably smart guy, a guy who'd had more than his fair share of gorgeous women, but this one had him tied up in knots.

Not.

Cool.

Thinking that he needed separation from her before he did something stupid—not that this entire evening hadn't been anything but one long stupidity—he reached across her and pushed her door open. Jaci seemed as eager to get away from him as he was from her, and she quickly scrambled out of the cab, giving him a superexcellent flash of a long, supple leg and the white garter holding up a thigh-high stocking. He felt the rush of blood to his groin and had to physically restrain himself from bolting after her and finding out whether the rest of her lingerie was up to the fantastic standard her garters set.

Ryan banged the back of his head on the seat as he watched Jaci walk toward the doormen standing on the steps of her building. She was trying to kill him, mentally and sexually.

It was the only explanation he could come up with.

Jaci, vibrating with fury, stood outside Ryan's swanky apartment building in Lenox Hill and stormed into the lobby, startling the dozy concierge behind the desk. He blinked at her and rubbed his hand over his face before lifting his hefty bulk to his feet.

"Help you?"

Jaci forced herself to unclench her jaw so that she could speak. "Please tell Ryan Jackson that Jaci Brookes-Lyon is here to see him."

Deputy Dog Doorman looked doubtful. "It's pretty late, miss. Is he expecting you?"

Jaci's molars ground together. "Just call him. Please?"

She received another uncertain look but he reached for the phone and dialed an extension. Within twenty seconds she was told that Ryan had agreed to see her—how kind of him!—and she was directed to the top floor.

"What number?" she demanded, turning on her spiked heel, wishing that she'd changed out of the dress she'd worn to the ballet before she'd stormed out of her apartment to confront him in his.

"No number. Mr. Jackson's apartment is on the top floor, *is* the top floor." The doorman sighed at her puzzled expression. "He has the penthouse apartment, miss."

"The penthouse?"

"Mr. Jackson recently purchased one of the most sought-after residences in the city, ma'am. Ten thousand square feet, four bedrooms with a wraparound terrace. Designer finishes, with crown moldings, high ceilings and custom herringbone floors," the concierge proudly explained.

"Good for him," Jaci muttered and headed for the elevator, the doorman on her heels. At the empty elevator, the doorman keyed in a code on the control panel on the wall and gestured her inside. "The elevator opens directly into his apartment, so guests need to be authorized to go up."

Whatever, Jaci thought, as the doors started to close.

"Have a good evening, miss."

She heard the words slide between the almost closed doors and she knew that she was about to have anything but. She'd been heading up to her apartment, intending to lick her wounds, when she'd suddenly felt intensely angry. It made her skin prickle and her throat tighten. How dare Ryan treat her as if she was something he'd caught on the bottom of his shoe? He'd refused to let her speak, had ignored her pleas to allow her to explain and had acted as if she were an empty-headed bimbo who should be grateful to spend any time she could in his exalted presence. And how stupid was he to challenge Leroy like that? It was entirely possible that he'd decimated any chance of Leroy funding *Blown Away* with his harshly uttered comments… And he accused *her* of acting rashly!

Unable to enter her apartment and stay there like a good little woman, she'd headed downstairs, hailed a cab and headed for Ryan's apartment, seething the whole way.

Maybe he could afford to let *Blown Away* blow away but she couldn't! She wasn't going to allow him to lose this chance to show the world, her family—to show herself—that she could be successful, too. It was a good script and she was determined that the world would see it!

Jaci released her tightly bunched hands and flexed her fingers; for an intensely smart man, Ryan could be amazingly stupid. And Jaci was going to tell him so—no man was going to get away with dismissing her again. She didn't care if he was her boss, or her fake boyfriend or her almost, albeit fake, fiancé. There was too much at stake: the film, her career and, most important right now, her pride.

Jaci rested her forehead against the oak-paneled interior of the elevator.

Unlike in her arguments with Clive, this time she would scream and shout. She'd do anything to be heard, dammit! And Ryan, that bossy, alpha, sexy sod, was going to get it with both barrels! Jaci had barely completed that thought when the elevator doors opened and she was looking into Ryan's living room, which was filled with comfortable couches and huge artwork. He stood in front of the mantel, and despite her anger, Jaci felt the slap of attraction. How could she not since he looked so rough and tough in his white dress shirt that showed off the breadth of his shoulders, his pants perfectly tailored to show off his lean waist and hips, his long, muscled legs.

The top two buttons of the shirt were open and the ends of his bow tie lay against his chest, and she wanted her hands there, on his chest, under his shirt, feeling that warm, masculine skin.

Focus. She wasn't here to have sex with him…but,

dear God with all his angels and archangels, she wanted to. She wanted to as she wanted her heart to keep beating.

If she was a man at least she would have the excuse of thinking with the little head, but because she was a woman she was out of luck.

"What do you want, Jaci?" Ryan demanded, jamming his hands into his suit pockets.

You. I want you. So much.

Jaci shook her head to dislodge that thought. This wasn't about a tumble, this was about the way he had treated her. Her third-grade teacher, Mrs. Joliet, was correct: *Jacqueline is too easily distracted.* Nothing, it seemed, had changed.

Jaci licked her lips.

"God, will you stop doing that?" Ryan demanded, his harsh voice cutting through the dense tension between him.

"What?" Jaci demanded, not having a clue what he was talking about. Her eyes widened as he stalked toward her, all fierce determination and easy grace, his eyes on her mouth.

"Licking your lips, biting your lip! That's my job." He grabbed her arms and jerked her up onto her toes. It was such a caveman-like action, but she couldn't help the thrill she felt when her chest slammed into his and her nipples pushed into his chest. If she wasn't such a sap she would be protesting about him treating her like a ditsy heroine in a romcom movie, but right now she didn't care. She was pressed so close to him that a beam of light couldn't pass through the space between them, and his mouth was covering hers.

And, God, then her world tipped over and flipped inside out. The kisses she'd shared with him before were a pale imitation of the passion she could taste on the tongue that swept inside her mouth, that she could feel in the hand that made a possessive sweep over her back, in the appreciative, low groans that she could hear in the back of his throat. In a small, rarely used part of her brain— the only cluster of brain cells that weren't overwhelmed by this fantastically smoking-hot kiss—she was in awe of the fact that Ryan wanted her like this.

It almost seemed as if kissing her, touching her, was more important to him than breathing. Actually, Jaci agreed, breathing was highly overrated. Her hands drifted up his chest, skimmed the warm skin beneath the collar of his shirt and wound around the back of his strong neck, feeling his heat, his strength. Then his hand covered her breast and he rubbed his palm across her nipple and, together with feeling the steel pipe that was pressing into her stomach, those last few brain cells shut down.

Ryan jerked his head back and, when she met them, his light eyes glittered down at her. "So, we're engaged, right?"

Jaci half shrugged. "Probably. At least we will be, in the eyes of the world, when the news breaks in a few hours."

"Well, in that case…" Ryan bent his knees and ran his hands up the outside of her thighs, her dress billowing over his forearms. "It's a damn good excuse to do this."

Jaci gasped as he played with the lace tops of her garters, danced up and across her hip bone and slid down to cover her bare butt cheek.

"Garters and a thong. I've died and gone to heaven," Ryan muttered, sliding his fingers under that thin cord.

Ryan sucked the soft spot where her jaw and neck

met, and she whimpered in delight. "God, Ryan…is this a good idea?"

Ryan pulled his head up and frowned down at her. "Who the hell knows? But if I'm going to be bagged and tagged, then I'm going to get something out of the deal. Stop playing with my hair and put your hands on me, Jace. I'm dying here."

Jaci did as she was told and she placed her hand flat against his sex. He jumped and groaned and she wanted more. She wanted him inside her, filling her, stretching her…but she had to be sensible.

"Just sex?" she asked, unable to stop her hand from pulling down the zipper to his pants and sliding on inside. She pushed down his underwear and there he was, hot and pulsing and hard and…oh, God, his hands were between her legs and he'd found her. Found that most magical, special, make-her-crazy spot…

"Yeah, one night to get this out of our systems. You okay with that? One night, no strings, no expectations of more?"

How was she supposed to think when his fingers were pushing their way inside? Her thumb rubbed his tip and she relished the groan she pulled from him. They were still fully dressed yet she was so damn close to gushing all over his hand. If he moved his thumb back to her hot nub, she'd lose it. Right here, right now.

"I'm supposed to be fighting with you right now," Jaci wailed.

Ryan responded by covering her mouth with his. After swiping his tongue across the indents her teeth marks made, he lifted his head to speak. "We can fight later. So, are we good? If not, now is the time to say no, and you'd better do it fast."

His words and attitude were tough but she couldn't miss the tension she felt in his body, in the way his arms tightened his hold on her, as if he didn't want to let her go. She should say no; it was the clever thing to do. She couldn't form the word, so she encased him in her fist and slid her hand up and then down his shaft in a low, sensuous slide.

Ryan responded by using his free hand to twist the thin rope of her underwear. She felt it rip, felt the quick tug, and then the fabric drifted down her leg to fall onto her right foot.

"This dress is killing me," he muttered, trying to pull the long layers up so that he could get as close to her as possible, while nudging her backward to the closest wall. She wasn't this person, Jaci thought. She didn't have sex up against a wall, she didn't scream and moan and sigh. She'd never been the person to make her lovers shout and groan and curse.

But, unless she was having a brilliant, mother of a hallucination, she was being that person right now. And... yay!

"It would be a lot easier if we just stripped," Jaci suggested, feeling the cool wall against her back. She leaned forward to push Ryan's pants and underwear down his thighs.

"That'll take too long." Ryan leaned his chest into hers, gripped the back of her thighs and lifted her. With unerring accuracy, his head found her channel and he slid along her, causing her to let out a low shriek of pleasure. "I can't wait for you, I can't leave...but God, we need a condom."

Jaci banged her head against the wall as he probed

her entrance. "On the pill and I've been tested for every STD under the sun," she muttered.

"I'm clean, too." Ryan choked the words out.

"I need you now. No more talking, no more fighting, just you and…" She lifted her hips and there he was, inside her, stretching her, filling her, completing her.

Ryan's mouth met hers and his tongue mimicked the movement of his hips, sliding in and out, leaving no part of her unexplored. Jaci felt hyperaware, as if her every sense was jacked up to maximum volume. She yanked his shirt up and ran her hands over his chest, around his ribs and down his strong back, digging her nails into his buttocks when he tilted his hips and went even deeper. She cried out and he yelled, and then suddenly she was riding a white-hot wave. In that moment of magical release, she felt connected to all the feminine energy in the world and she was its conduit.

She felt powerful and uninhibited and so damn wild. When she came back to herself, back to the wall and to Ryan's face buried in her neck, his broad hands were still holding her thighs.

Jaci dropped her face into his neck and touched her tongue to the cord in his neck. "Take me to bed, Ryan. We can fight later."

"I can do that, and we most likely will," Ryan muttered as he pulled out of her and allowed her to slide down his body. He kicked off his pants and pulled her, her hair and dress and mind tangled, down the hallway to his bedroom. "But, for now, I can't wait any longer… I've got to see you naked."

Seven

Jaci pushed back the comforter and left the bed, glancing down at her naked body. Clothes would be nice and she wrinkled her nose at the pile of fabric in a heap on the floor, just on this side of the door. Pulling that on was going to be horrible, as was the walk of shame she'd be doing later as she headed back to her apartment in a wrinkled dress and with messy hair.

Then Jaci saw the T-shirt and pair of boxer shorts on Ryan's pillow. They hadn't been there earlier so Ryan must have left them for her to wear. Sweet of him, she thought, pulling the T-shirt over her head. It was enormous on her, the hem coming to midthigh. It was long enough for her to be decent without wearing underwear but there was no way that she was going commando. She couldn't even pull on the thong she wore last night since Ryan had, literally, ripped it off her. Sighing, she pulled up his boxers, rolling the waistband a couple of times until she was certain they wouldn't fall off her hips.

"Mornin'."

Jaci yelped and spun around, her mouth drying at the sight of a rumpled, unshaven Ryan standing in the doorway, dressed only in a faded pair of jeans, zipped but not buttoned. She was so used to seeing him impeccably, stylishly dressed that observing him looking like a scruffy cowboy had her womb buzzing. She started to bite her lip and abruptly stopped.

"Hi," she murmured, unable to keep the heat from flaring on her cheeks. She'd kissed those rock-hard abs, raked her fingers up those hard thighs, taken a nip of those thick biceps. And if he gave her one hint that he'd like her to do it again, she'd Flash Gordon herself to his side.

But Ryan kept his face impassive. "Coffee?"

"Yeah." Jaci made herself move toward the door and took the cup from his hand, being careful not to touch him. She took a grateful sip, sighed and met his eyes. His shoulder was against the door frame and he looked dark and serious, and she quickly realized that playtime was over. "I guess you want to talk?"

What about? Being engaged? Leroy? The script? The amazing sex they'd shared?

"Since we are the leading story in the entertainment world, I think that would be a very good idea." Ryan peeled himself from the door and walked down the hallway. Well, that answered that question. Good thing, because while she knew that she was old enough to have a one-night stand with her fake boyfriend, she doubted that she could talk about it. Jaci followed, trying but not succeeding at keeping her eyes off his tight, masculine butt.

"I have a million messages on my mobile and in my inbox, from reporters and friends, asking if it's true," Ryan said, heading across his living room to the luxurious open-plan kitchen. He grabbed the coffeepot and refilled a cup that had been sitting on the island in the center of the kitchen. Judging by the fact that the coffeepot was nearly empty, he'd been up for a while and this was his third or fourth cup.

Jaci took a sip from her own cup of coffee and wrinkled her nose at the bitter, dark taste. "What do you want to do? Deny or confirm?"

Ryan rested his bottom against the kitchen counter and pushed a hand through his hair. "I suppose that depends on your explanation on why you made such an asinine comment."

Jaci swallowed down her retort and another sip of coffee. Taking a seat on one of the stools that lined the breakfast bar, she put her cup on the granite surface and placed her chin in the palm of her hand. "I tried to explain last night."

"Last night there was only one thing I wanted from you and it wasn't an explanation." He waved his coffee cup. "Go."

Jaci rubbed her forehead with her fingertips in an effort to ease the headache that was gaining traction. Too much sex and not enough sleep. "Leroy hired a PI to investigate me, and you, by the way. He obviously found out about my broken engagement and was questioning how quickly I moved on."

Ryan's focus on her face didn't waver. "Okay. I presume that you had a very good reason for leaving the politician?"

"You still haven't done your own digging?" Jaci asked, surprised.

"I'm waiting for your version," Ryan replied. "Not important now… Go back to explaining how we got engaged."

"Right." Jaci sipped and sighed. "I asked Banks why me, what this was all about. I mean, this makes no sense to me… I'm nothing special. He said that it didn't matter why he wanted me, only that he always gets what he wants. That he's now using me to get a handle on you." Jaci ran a fingertip around the rim of her cup. "I thought that we needed to take me out of the equation, to remove me as a pawn. That can only happen if we break up or if he thinks that the relationship between us is more serious than he realized. So I thought that if I told him that we were thinking of marriage—thinking of, not that we were engaged—he'd back off."

Ryan shook his head. "Marriage, fidelity, faithfulness mean nothing to him. He's married to a sweet, sexy, lovely woman whom he treats like trash. You just handed him more ammunition to mess with me by suggesting we're that deeply involved. You poured blood into the water and the sharks are going to come and investigate."

Jaci looked bleak. "You mean the press."

"Yep. There's a reason why I keep a low profile, Jaci, and I've appeared more in the press since I've met you than in the last few years." Ryan banged his coffee cup as he placed it on the counter and rubbed the back of his neck. "They were relentless when Ben died, and I had so much else I was dealing with that the last thing I needed was to read the flat-out fiction they were printing in the papers. And the last thing I need right now is dealing with the press as I deal with Banks."

Jaci tilted her head. "And you smacked him down last night... Are you worried about the consequences? Think he might bail?"

Ryan lifted a powerful shoulder in an uneasy shrug. "We'll have to wait and see."

"Wait and see?" Jaci demanded, her face flushing. "Ryan, this is my career we're talking about, my big break. You might be able to afford to let this project go down the toilet but I can't. If I have any chance of being recognized as a serious scriptwriter, I need this film to be produced, I need it to be successful."

"I know that!" Ryan slapped his hands on his hips and scowled at her. "I don't want this project to fail, either, Jaci. I'll lose millions of my own money, money that I've paid into the development of this film. It'll take a good while for me to recover that money if I lose it."

"This is such a tangled mess," Jaci said in a low voice. She flipped him a look. "I shouldn't have kissed you. It was an impulsive gesture that has had huge consequences."

Ryan looked at her for a long time before replying. "Don't beat yourself up too much. I am also to blame. You didn't deepen that kiss, I did, and I told Leroy that you were my girlfriend."

"Okay, I'll happily let you accept most of the blame."

"*Some* of the blame. It wasn't my crazy idea to say that we were thinking of getting married." Ryan shook his head at her when she opened her mouth to argue. "Enough arguing, okay? I need sustenance."

Ryan walked over to the double-door, stainless steel fridge and yanked open a door and stared inside. "You're wrong, you know," he said, and Jaci had to strain to hear his words.

"Since I've been wrong so many times lately you're going to have to be more specific," Jaci told him.

"About not being special." Ryan slammed the door shut and turned around, slowly and unwillingly and, it had to be said, empty-handed. "You are the dream within the dream."

Jaci frowned. "Sorry?"

Ryan cleared his throat and she was amazed that this man, so confident in business and in bed, could look and sound this uneasy. "Banks has everything money can buy except he wants what money can't buy. Happiness, normality, love."

"But you've just said that he has a stunning, lovely wife—"

"Thea was a top supermodel and Banks knows that she is far too good for him." Ryan folded his arms and rocked on his heels. "Look, forget about it…"

Jaci shook her head, thinking that she needed to know where he was going with this. "Nope, your turn to spill. Are you telling me that I am more suited to Banks than his gorgeous, sweet, stunning wife?"

"Jesus, no!" Ryan looked horrified and he cursed. "But he knows that you are different from the women he normally runs into."

Oh, different, yay. Generally in her experience that meant less than. "Super," she said drily.

"Look, you're real."

"Real?" Jaci asked, confused.

"Yeah. Despite your almost aristocratic background, you seem to have your feet planted firmly on the ground. You aren't a gold digger or a slut or a party girl or a diva. You're as normal as it comes."

"Is normal higher up on the attractiveness ladder than real?" She just couldn't tell.

Ryan muttered a curse. "You are determined to misunderstand me. I'm just trying to explain why your openness, lack of bitchiness and overall genuineness is helluva attractive."

"Oh, so you *do* think that I am attractive?" Jaci muttered and heard Ryan's sharp intake of breath.

"No, of course not. I just made love to you all last night because I thought you were a troll." Ryan sent her one of those male looks that clearly stated he thought she was temporarily bat-lolly insane.

"Oh." Jaci felt heat creep across her face. She noticed him clenching and releasing his fists as if he were trying to stop himself from reaching for her. And in a flash she could feel the thump-thump-thump of her own heart, could hear the sound as clearly as she could read the desire in his eyes.

Ryan Jackson hadn't had nearly enough of her or, she had to admit, her of him. One more time, Jaci told herself, she could give herself the present of having, holding, feeling Ryan again. He wanted her, she wanted him, so what was the problem?

Career, Banks, sleeping with your boss? Jaci ignored the sensible angel on her shoulder and slid off her chair, her body heating from the inside out and her stomach and womb taking turns doing tumbles and backflips inside her body.

"One more time," she muttered as she stroked her hand up Ryan's chest to grip his neck and pull his mouth down to hers.

"Why do I suspect that's not going to be enough?" Ryan muttered, his lips a fraction from hers.

"It has to be. Shut up and kiss me," Jaci demanded, lifting herself up on her toes.

Ryan's lips curved against hers. "Just as long as we won't be married when we come up for air."

"Funny." Jaci just got the words out before Ryan took possession of her mouth, and then no words were needed.

Jaci, sitting in Ryan's office four days later, was struggling to keep her pretend-you-haven't-licked-me-there expression, especially now that their conversation had moved on from discussing the script changes he and Thom wanted. She hadn't seen Ryan since she left his apartment the morning after the ballet; he hadn't called, he hadn't texted.

And that was the way it should be, she told herself. What they'd shared was purely bedroom based. It meant nothing more than two adults succumbing to a primal desire that had driven mankind for millennia. He'd wanted her, she'd wanted—God, that was such a tame word for the need he'd aroused in her!—him and that was all it was.

Then why did she want to ask him why his eyes looked bleak? Why did she want to climb into his lap, place her face into his neck and tell him that it would all work out? She wanted to massage the knots out of his neck, smooth away the frown between his heavy brows, kiss away the bracket that appeared next to his mouth. He was off-the-charts stressed and it was all her fault.

She'd put his relationship with his investor on the line. It was amazing that she was still discussing script changes, that he hadn't fired her scrawny ass.

"Have you heard anything from Banks yet?" she demanded, pulling her gaze away from the view of the Hudson River.

Ryan looked startled at the sudden subject change. He exchanged a long look with Thom and after their silent communication, Thom stood up. "Actually…"

Thom lifted a hand and he ambled to the door. "You can explain. Later."

Jaci's eyebrows rose. "Explain what?"

Ryan tapped the nib of a pen on the pad of paper next to his laptop. "We've been invited to join a dinner on a luxury yacht tonight. The invitation came from Banks's office. Apparently Leroy's just bought himself an Ajello superyacht and this is its initial voyage. Lucky Leroy, those are only the best yachts in the world."

Jaci stood up and walked toward the floor-to-ceiling window, shoving her hands into the back pockets of her pants.

"I like your outfit," Ryan commented.

Jaci looked down at the deep brown leather leggings she'd teamed with a flowing white top and multiple strands of ethnic beads. It was nice to wear something other than black, she thought, and it made her feel warm and squirmy that Ryan approved. "I must be doing something right because a random man complimented my outfit in a coffee shop yesterday, as well."

"Honey, any man under dead would've noticed those stupendous legs under that flirty skirt." She saw the flare of heat in his eyes and looked down at her feet encased in knee-high leather boots. Damn but she really wanted to walk over to him and kiss him senseless. Her fingers tingled with the need to touch and her legs parted as if… Dear Lord, this was torture!

"I'm glad that the furor over our possible engagement

has died down," she said, trying to get her mind to stop remembering how fantastic Ryan looked naked.

"It was nothing that my PR firm couldn't handle," Ryan said, leaning back in his chair and placing his hands on his flat stomach. "As of the columns this morning, we're still seeing each other, but any talk of marriage is for the very distant future."

Jaci felt her shoulders drop and quickly pulled them up again. She had no reason to feel let down, no reason at all. She wasn't looking for a relationship, not even a pretend one. She'd been engaged, had talked incessantly about marriage—and what did she get out of that? Humiliation and hurt. Yeah, no thanks.

"As for Leroy's silence, you know what they say, no news is good news." Ryan picked up a file from his desk and flipped it open.

"Shouldn't you call him, say something, do something?" Jaci demanded, and his eyes rose at her vehement statement.

Ryan closed his file and leaned back in his chair. "It's a game, Jaci, and I'm playing it," he replied, linking his fingers on his stomach. Then his eyes narrowed. "You don't like the way I'm playing it?"

"I don't know the flipping rules!" Jaci snapped back. "And it's my future that's at stake, too. I have a lot to lose, but I can't do anything to move this along."

Ryan frowned at her outburst. "It's not the end of the world, Jace. Don't you and your siblings have a big trust fund that's at your disposal? It's not like you'll be out on the streets if this movie never gets produced. And you'll write other scripts, have other chances."

Could she tell him? Did she dare? She'd hinted at how important this was to her before, but maybe if he understood how crucial it really was, he'd understand why this situation was making her stress levels redline. And it wasn't as if he was a stranger; she had known him for years.

"This script means more to me than just a break into the industry, Ryan. It's more than that. It's more than my career or my future..." She saw him frown and wondered how she could explain the turbulent, churning emotions inside. "It's a symbol, a tipping point, a fork in the road."

She expected him to tell her to stop being melodramatic, but he just sat calmly and waited for her to continue. "You buying my script and offering me a job to work on *Blown Away* was—is—more than a career opportunity. It was the catalyst that propelled me into a whole new life." Jaci gestured to her notes on the desk. "That's all mine...my effort, my words, my script. This is something I did, without my parents' knowledge or without them pulling any strings. It's the divide between who I was before and who I am now. God, I am so not explaining this well."

"Stop editing yourself and just talk, Jace."

"On one side of the divide, I was the Brookes-Lyon child who drifted from job to job, who played at writing, maybe to get her mother's attention. Then I became Clive's fiancée and an object of press attention and I had to grow a spine, fast. I couldn't have survived what I did without it. When I left London, I vowed that I wasn't going to fade into the background again."

"Yeah, you used to do that as a kid. Your family would take over and dominate a room, a conversation, yet you wouldn't contribute a thing." His mouth twitched. "Now you won't shut up."

"It's because I'm different in New York!" Jaci stated, her face animated. "I'm better here. Happier, feistier!"

"I like feisty." Ryan murmured his agreement in a low voice, heat in the long, hot glance he sent her.

It was so hard to ignore the desire in his voice. But she had to. "I don't want to go backward, Ry. If I lose this opportunity..."

Ryan frowned at her and leaned forward. "Jaci, what you do is not who you are. You can still be feisty without the job."

Could she be? She didn't think so; Sassy Jaci needed to be successful. If she wasn't then she'd just be acting. She didn't want to skate through her life anymore. She wanted to live and feel and be this new Jaci. She *liked* this new Jaci.

Ryan pinned her to the floor with his intense blue-gray stare. "Have a little faith, Jace. It will all work out."

But what if it didn't? Who would she be if she couldn't be New York Jaci? She didn't know if she could reinvent herself again. She saw Ryan looking over his desk, saw his hand moving toward the folder he'd discarded minutes before and read the silent message. It was time to go back to work, so she started for the door.

Ryan's phone rang and he lifted his finger to delay her. "Hang on a sec. We still need to talk about the yacht thing tonight."

Oh, bats, she'd forgotten about that. Jaci stopped next to his desk.

"Hey, Jax." The voice of Ryan's PA floated through the speakers of the phone. "Jaci's mother is on the phone and she sounds...determined. I think Jaci needs to take this."

"Sure, put her through."

Jaci shot up and pulled her hand across her throat in a

slashing motion. Dear Lord, the last person in the world she wanted to talk to was her mother. She still hadn't told them that she was working as a scriptwriter, that she was pseudo-dating Ryan…

"Morning, Priscilla."

Jaci glared at him and grabbed the pen out of his hand and scribbled across the writing pad in front of him. *I'm NOT here*; she underlined the *not* three times.

He cocked an eyebrow at her and quickly swung his right leg around the back of her knees to cage her between his legs. Jaci sent him her death-ray glare, knowing that she couldn't struggle without alerting her mother to her presence. As it was she was certain that Priscilla could hear her pounding heart and shaky breathing as she stood trapped between Ryan's legs.

"Ryan, darling boy." Priscilla's voice was as rich and aristocratic as ever. "How are you? It's been so long since we've seen you. I can't wait to see you at Neil's wedding next weekend."

Jaci slapped her hand against her forehead and stifled her gasp of horror. She'd forgotten all about Neil's blasted wedding. It was next weekend? Good Lord! How had that happened?

Jaci quickly drew a hanging man on the pad, complete with a bulging tongue, and she felt the rumble of laughter pass through Ryan as he exchanged genialities with her mother, quickly explaining that Jaci had just left his office. Ryan was talking about his duties as best man when she felt him grip the waistband of her pants and pull her down to sit on his hard thigh. Jaci sent him a startled look. Being this close was so damn tempting…

Oh, who was she kidding? Being in the same room as Ryan was too damn tempting. Jaci closed her eyes as his hand moved up her back and gripped the nape of her neck. His other hand briefly rested on her thigh before he pulled the pen from her hand and scribbled on the pad with his left hand. Huh, he was left-handed… She'd forgotten.

Jaci looked down at the pad, and it took a moment for her to decipher his scrawl. *Why don't you want to talk to your mother?*

"Yes, I have my suit and Neil told me, very clearly and very often, that he didn't want a stag party. He couldn't take the time away from work."

Jaci grabbed another pen from his container of stationery and scribbled her reply. *Because she doesn't know what I am doing in New York and that we're…you know.*

Why not? & what does "you know" mean? Sleeping together? Pretending to date?

Jaci kept half an ear on her mother's ramblings. After nearly thirty years of practice, she knew when she'd start slowing down, and they had at least a minute.

All of it, she replied. *She—they—just think that I'm licking my wounds. They don't take my work—*

Jaci stopped writing and stared at the page. Ryan tapped the page with the pen in a silent order for her to finish her sentence. She sent him a small smile and lifted her shoulders in an it-doesn't-matter shrug. Ryan's glare told her it did.

"Anyway, what on earth is this nonsense I'm reading in the press about you and Jaci?"

Ah, her mother was upset. Jaci, perfectly comfortable on Ryan's knee, sucked in her cheeks and stared at a point beyond Ryan's shoulder.

"What have you heard?" Ryan asked, his tone wary. The hand moved away from her neck to draw large, comforting circles on her back. Jaci felt herself relax with every pass of his hand.

"I have a list," Priscilla stated. Of course she did. Priscilla would want to make sure that she didn't forget anything. "Firstly, is she working as a scriptwriter for you?"

"She is."

"And you're paying her?" There was no missing the astonishment in her voice.

"I am." Jaci heard the bite in those two words as he drew three question marks on the pad.

Not serious writing, Jaci replied. Ryan's eyes narrowed at her response, and she felt her stomach heat at his annoyance at her statement. Nice to be appreciated.

"She's a very talented writer," Ryan added. "She must have got that from you."

Thanks, Jaci wrote as his words distracted her mother and she launched into a monologue about her latest book, set in fourteenth-century England. Jaci jumped when she felt his hand on the bare skin of her back. His fingers rubbed the bumps on her spine and Jaci felt lightning bolts dance where he touched her.

Concentrate! she wrote.

Can do two things at once. God, your skin is so soft. We're not doing this again!

And you smell so good.

"Anyway, I'm getting off the subject. Are you and Jaci engaged or not?" Priscilla demanded.

"Not," Ryan answered, his eyes on Jaci's mouth. She knew that he wanted to kiss her and, boy, it was difficult to resist the desire in his eyes, knowing the amount of pleasure he was capable of giving her.

"Good, because after that louse she was engaged to, she needs some time to regroup. *That stuffed cloak-bag of guts!*" Ryan's eyebrows flew upward at Priscilla's venomous statement. *Shakespeare*, Jaci scribbled. *Henry IV.*

"Jaci was far too good for him!" Jaci jerked her eyes away from Ryan's to stare at the phone. Really? And why couldn't her mother have told *her* this?

"That business with the Brazilian madam was just too distasteful for words, and so stupid. Did he really think he wouldn't get caught?"

Brazilian? Madam?

My ex liked a little tickle and a lot of slap.

Ryan stared down at the page before lifting his eyes back to Jaci's rueful face. "Jesus," he muttered.

"I do hope that she got herself tested after all of that but I can't ask her," Priscilla stated in a low voice. "We don't have that type of relationship. And that's my fault."

Jaci's mouth fell open at that statement. Her mother wished that they were closer? Seriously?

"And what's going on between you? Are you dating? Is it serious? Are you sleeping together?" Priscilla demanded.

Jaci opened her mouth to tell her that it was none of her damn business, but Ryan's hand was quicker and he covered her mouth with his hand. She glowered at him and tried to tug his hand away.

"It's complicated, Priscilla. I'm involved in a deal and, bizarrely, I needed a girlfriend to help me secure it. Jaci stepped up to the plate." Ryan kept his hand on her mouth. "It's all pretend."

"Well, I'm looking at a photograph of the two of you and it doesn't look like either of you are pretending to me."

Ryan dropped his hand but not his eyes. "We're good actors, it seems," he eventually replied.

"Huh. Well, I hope this mess gets sorted out soon," Priscilla said. "Not that I would mind if you and Jaci were involved. I have always liked you."

"Thank you," Ryan replied. "The sentiment is returned."

Such a suck-up, Jaci scribbled and gasped when his arm pulled her against his chest. Against her hip she could feel his hard erection, and she really couldn't help nestling her face into his neck and inhaling his scent. Damn, she could just drift away, right here, right now, in his arms.

"I must go. Take care of my baby, Ryan."

Ryan's arms tightened around Jaci and she sighed. "Will do, Priscilla."

"Bye, Ryan. Bye, my darling Jaci."

"Bye, Mom," Jaci replied lazily, the fingers of her left hand diving between the buttons of his dress shirt to feel his skin. Then her words sank in and she shot up and looked at Ryan in horror as the call disconnected.

"She knew that I was here. The witch!"

Ryan just laughed.

Eight

That evening, Leroy, too busy showing off his amazing yacht, ignored them, and Ryan was more than happy with that. He and Jaci stood at the back of the boat, where there was less of a crowd, and watched the city skyline transition from day to night. Dusk was a magical time of the day, Ryan thought, resting his forearms on the railing and letting his beer bottle dangle from his fingers over the Hudson River. It had the ability to soothe, to suggest that something bolder and brighter was waiting around the next corner. Or maybe that was the woman standing next to him.

Ryan stood up and looked at her. Tonight's dress was a frothy concoction with beads up top, no back and a full skirt that ended midthigh. He wanted to call it a light green but knew that if he had to ask Jaci to tell him what color it was she'd say that it was pistachio or sea foam or something ridiculous. Equally ridiculous was his desire to walk her down to one of the staterooms below deck and peel her out of it. His nights had been consumed with thoughts and dreams—awake and asleep—about her. He wanted her again, a hundred times more. He'd never—he ran his hand over his face—*craved* anyone before.

Ryan rubbed the back of his neck and was grateful that his heavy sigh was covered by the sound of the engine as it pushed the yacht and its fifty-plus guests through the water. Jaci had him tied up in every sailor knot imaginable. In his office this morning, it had taken every atom of his being to push her out of his lap so that he could get back to work. He was watching his multimillion-dollar deal swirling in the toilet bowl, Jaci's career—her big break and, crazily, her self-worth—was on the line, and all he could think about was when next he could get her into bed.

Despite wanting her as he wanted his next breath, he also wanted to go back to being the uncomplicated person he'd been before Jaci hurtled into his life. And it had been uncomplicated: he had an ongoing love–hate relationship with his dead brother, a hate–hate relationship with his father and, thanks to Kelly's lack of fidelity, a not-getting-involved attitude to women.

Simple, when you looked at it like that.

But Jaci made him feel stuff he didn't want to feel. She made him remember what his life had been like before Ben's death. He'd been so damn happy, so confident and so secure in the belief that all was right with his world. He'd accepted that his father was a hemorrhoid but that he could live with it; at the time his best mate was also his brother and he was engaged to the most beautiful girl in the world. He was starting to taste success…

And one evening it all disappeared. Without warning. And he learned that nothing lasted forever and no one stuck around for the long haul. It was just a truth of his life.

God, get a grip, Jackson. You sound like a whiny, bitchy teenager. Ryan turned his attention back to Jaci, who'd been content to stand quietly at his side, her shoulder pressed into his, her light perfume dancing on the breeze.

"So, whips and chains, huh?" It was so much easier to talk about Jaci's failures than his own.

Jaci sent him a startled look and when his words made sense, her expression turned rueful. "Well, I'm not so sure about the chains but there definitely were whips involved."

Dipstick, Ryan thought, placing his hand in the center of Jaci's back. She sent him a tentative smile but her expressive eyes told him that she'd been emotionally thrown under a bus. He nodded to a padded bench next to him and guided Jaci to it, ordering another glass of wine for Jaci and a whiskey for himself. Jaci sat down, crossed one slim leg over the other and stared at the delicate, silver high heel on her foot.

"Talk to me," Ryan gently commanded. He was incredibly surprised when she did just that.

"I was impressed by him and, I suppose, impressed by the idea that this rising-star politician—and he really was, Ryan—wanted to be with me. He's charismatic and charming and so very, very bright."

"He sounds like a lightbulb."

His quip didn't bring the smile to her face he'd hoped to see. "Did you love him?"

Jaci took a long time to answer. "I loved the fact that

he said that he loved me. That everyone seemed to adore him and, by extension, adored me. Up to and including my family."

Another of the 110 ways family can mess with your head, Ryan thought. It had been a long time since he'd interacted with the Brookes-Lyon clan but he remembered thinking that, while they were great individually, together they were a force of nature and pretty much unbearable. "My family loved him. He slid right on in. He was as smart and as driven as them, and my approval rating with them climbed a hundred points when I brought him home and then skyrocketed when I said yes to getting married."

The things we do for parental and familial approval, Ryan thought with an internal shake of his head. "But he wasn't the Prince Charming you thought he was."

Jaci lifted one shoulder in a shrug. "We got engaged and it was a big deal, the press went wild. He was a tabloid darling before but together with the fact that he was gaining political power, he became the one to watch. And they really watched him."

Ryan frowned, trying to keep up. "The press?"

"Yeah. And their doggedness paid off," Jaci said in a voice that was pitched low but threaded with embarrassment and pain. "He was photographed in a club chatting up a Brazilian blonde, looking very cozy. The photos were inappropriate but nothing that couldn't be explained away."

She pushed her bangs out of her eyes and sighed. "About two weeks after the photographs appeared, I was at his flat waiting for him to come home. I'd prepared this romantic supper, I'd really pulled out the stops. He was running late so I decided to work on some wedding plans while I waited. I needed to contact a band who'd play at the reception and I knew that Clive had the address in his contacts, so I opened up his email program."

Ryan, knowing what was coming, swore.

"Yep. There were about sixteen unread emails from a woman and every one had at least four photos attached." Jaci closed her eyes as the images danced across her brain. "They were explicit. She was known as the Mistress of Pain."

He winced.

Jaci stared across the river to the lights of Staten Island. When she spoke again, her words were rushed, as if she just wanted to tell her story and get it done. "I knew that this could blow up in our faces so I confronted Clive. We agreed that we would quietly, with as little fuss as possible, call it quits. Before we could, the story broke that he was seeing a dominatrix and the bomb blew up in our faces." Ryan lifted his eyebrows as Jaci flicked her fingers open, mimicking the action of a bomb detonating.

"Ouch."

"Luckily, a month later a crazy producer made me an offer to work in New York as a scriptwriter and I jumped at the chance to get the hell out of, well, hell."

"And you didn't tell your family that you had a job?"

"It's not like they would've heard me, and if they did, they wouldn't have taken it seriously. They'd think my writing is something I play at while I'm looking to find what I'm really going to do with the rest of my life."

Ryan heard the strains of a ballad coming from the band on the front deck and stood up. Pulling Jaci to her feet, he placed his hand on her hip and gripped her other hand and started to sway. She was in his arms, thank God. He rubbed his chin through her hair and bent his head so that his mouth was just above her ear. He thought about telling her how sorry he was that she'd been hurt, that she deserved none of it, how much he wanted to kiss her...everywhere. Instead, he gathered her closer by placing both his hands on her back and pulled her into him.

"For a bunch of highly intellectual people, your family is as dumb as a bag of ostrich feathers when it comes to you."

Jaci tipped her head and he saw appreciation shining in those deep, hypnotic eyes. "That's the nicest thing you've ever said to me."

He was definitely going to have to try harder, Ryan thought as he held her close and slowly danced her across the deck.

Leroy didn't bother to engage with them, Jaci thought, when they were back in the taxi and making their way from the luxury marina in Jersey City back to Manhattan. She wasn't sure whether that was a good or a bad thing.

She sighed, frustrated. "God, the business side of moviemaking gives me a headache."

"It gives me a freakin' migraine," Ryan muttered. "I've got about a two-week window and then I need to decide whether to pull the plug on the project or not."

Two weeks? That was all? Jaci, hearing the stress in Ryan's voice, twisted her ring around her finger. Who could magic that much money out of thin air in less than two weeks? This was all her fault; if she hadn't kissed him in that lobby, if she hadn't gone to that stupid party, if she hadn't moved to New York... It was one thing messing up her own life, but she'd caused so much trouble for Ryan, this hard-eyed and hard-bodied man who didn't deserve any of this.

"I'm so, so sorry." Jaci rested her head on the window and watched the buildings fly past. "This is all my fault."

Ryan didn't respond and Jaci felt the knife of guilt dig a little deeper, twist a little more. She thought about apologizing again and realized that repeating the sentiment didn't change the facts. She couldn't rewrite the past. All she could do was try to manage the present. But there was little—actually nothing—that she could do to unravel this convoluted mess, and she knew that Ryan would tie her to a bedpost if he thought that there was a minuscule chance of her complicating the situation any further.

Out of the corner of her eye she saw him dig his slim cell phone out of the inner pocket of his gray jacket. He squinted at the display. His long fingers flew across the keypad and she saw the corners of his mouth twitch, the hint of a smile passing across his face.

Ryan lifted his eyes to look at her. "Your brother just reamed me a new one for sleeping with you."

Jaci ignored the swoop of her stomach, pushed away the memory of the way Ryan's arms bulged as he held himself above her, the warmth of his eyes as he slid on home. "He thinks that we're sleeping together?"

"Yep," Ryan responded. "And if you check your cell, you'll probably find a couple messages from the rest of your family." Ryan placed a hand on her thigh, and her breath hitched as his fingers drew patterns on her bare skin. "Priscilla has a very big mouth."

"Oh, dear Lord God in heaven." Jaci resisted the desire to slap her mouth against his and made herself ignore the heat in his eyes, the passion that flared whenever they were breathing the same air. She grabbed her evening bag, pulled out her own phone and groaned at the five missed calls and the numerous messages on their family group chat.

Oh, this was bad, this was very bad.

Jaci touched the screen to bring up the messages.

Meredith: You have some explaining to do, sunshine.

Priscilla: Screenwriting? Really? Since when? Why don't you tell me anything?

Ryan moved up the seat so that his thigh was pressed against hers, and her shoulder jammed into his arm. She inhaled his scent and when heat dropped into her groin, she shifted in the seat. Ryan moved her phone so that he could see the screen.

Neil: Ryan? I was expecting you to have coffee with him, not an affair!

Meredith: Admittedly, anyone is better than the moron, but I don't think you should be jumping into a relationship this quickly!

Archie: Ryan? Who the hell is Ryan?

Neil: My Yank friend from uni, Dad.

Archie: The Hollywood one? The pretty boy?

Jaci rubbed her fingertips across her forehead. Damn, the Atlantic Ocean might be between them but her family still managed to exacerbate her headache. She looked at Ryan and shrugged. "Well, you *are* pretty."

Ryan dug an elbow into her side. "Your opinion on how I look is a lot more important than your father's," he said, his tone low and oozing sex.

Jaci deliberately lifted her nose in a haughty gesture, her eyes twinkling. "You'll do."

Ryan squeezed her thigh in response. "I suppose I asked for that." He nodded to the phone in her hands. "So, what are you going to tell them?"

Jaci tapped her finger against her lips. "The same

thing you told my mother—that it was a pretend thing, that we aren't in a relationship, that this isn't going anywhere." She turned her head to look out the window. "Basically the truth."

Ryan's finger and thumb gripped her chin and turned her face to look at him. Jaci stifled a sigh at his gorgeous eyes and gripped her phone with both hands to keep them from diving into his hair, from rubbing his neck, his shoulders. Her mouth wanted to touch his, her legs wanted to climb onto his lap...

Ryan looked at her mouth and she felt his fingers tighten on her chin. He was fighting the urge to kiss her, as well, she realized. His rational side was barely winning and that realization made her feel powerful and feminine and so wanted. She'd never felt this desired. No man had ever looked at her the way Ryan was looking at her right now, right here.

"Your family is thinking that we are sleeping together," Ryan stated, his thumb moving up from her chin to stroke her full bottom lip.

Well, that was obvious. She glanced at her phone in confusion. "Well, yeah."

"Not that I give a rat's ass what your family thinks, but..."

Jaci felt her breath stop somewhere on the way to her lungs. "But?"

"Screw this, we don't need to explain this or justify this or make excuses for this."

For what? Jaci frowned, confused. "What are you trying, very badly, to say, Ryan?"

"I want you. I want you in my bed. Screw the fact that you work for me and the film and all the rest of the craziness. I just want you. Come home with me, Jace. Be mine for as long as this madness continues."

Be his. Two words, two syllables, but so powerful. How was she supposed to be sensible, to back away, to resist? She wasn't an angel and she definitely wasn't a saint. Jaci quickly justified the decision she was about to make. He wanted her, she—desperately—wanted him. They were both single and this was about sex and passion and lust... No love was required. They weren't hurting anyone...

If you fall in love with him, you'll hurt yourself.

Then I won't fall in love with him, Jaci told herself. But a little part of her doubted that statement and she pulled back, wondering if she shouldn't just take a breath and get oxygen to her brain. *You've been hurt enough*, that same cautious inner voice told her. And Ryan would take what was left of her battered heart and drop-kick it to the moon.

"I can't get enough of you," Ryan muttered before slanting his mouth over hers and pushing his tongue between her parted lips. One swipe, another lick and all doubts were gone, all hesitation burned away by the heat of his mouth, the passion she tasted on her tongue. His arm pushed down between her back and the seat, and his other hand held her head in place so that he commanded the kiss. And command he did, and Jaci followed him into that special, magical place where time stood still.

Under his touch... This was where she felt alive, powerful, connected to the universe and sure of her place in it. When she kissed him she felt confident and desired and potent. Like the best version of herself. Ryan's mouth left hers and he feathered openmouthed kisses across her cheekbone, along her jaw, down her neck. Jaci shivered when he tasted the hollow of her collarbone.

"We've got to stop making out in cabs," Ryan murmured against her skin.

"We've got to stop making out, full stop," Jaci tartly replied.

"News flash, honey, that's probably not going to happen." Jaci felt Ryan's lips curve into a smile against her neck. The backs of his fingers brushed her breast as he straightened and moved away from her, his expression regretful. He looked past her and Jaci finally noticed that they were parked outside Ryan's swish apartment building.

"Come inside with me, please."

How could she resist the plea in his eyes, the smidgen of anxiety she heard in his voice? Did he really think that she was strong enough to say no, that she was wise enough to walk away from this situation, to keep this as uncomplicated as it could possibly be? Well, no chance of that. Her brain thought that she should stay in the cab and have the driver deliver her home, but the need to erase the distance between them, to feel every naked inch of him, was overpowering. She wanted Ryan, she needed him. She was going to take him and have him take her.

The morning and its problems could look after themselves. Tonight was hers. He was hers. Jaci opened the door and left the cab, teetering on her heels as she spun around and held out her hand to Ryan.

"Take me to bed, Ry."

Ryan enjoyed women; he liked their curves, their soft-feeling, smooth skin, the small, delicate sounds they made when his touch gave them pleasure. He loved the sweet-spicy taste of their skin, their pretty toes, the way their tantalizing softness complemented his hard, rougher body.

Yeah, he liked women, but he adored Jaci, he thought as he slowly pulled her panties down her hips. Naked at last. Ryan, minus his jacket and black tie, was still dressed and liking the contrast. He dropped the froth of lace to the floor and sat on the side of the bed, his hand stroking her long thigh, watching how her small nipples puckered when he looked at them. He'd had more than his share of women but none of them reacted to his look as if it was a touch. There had never been this arc of desire connecting them. He'd never felt a driving need to touch anyone the way he wanted to touch her.

It was both terrifying and amazingly wonderful.

"What are you thinking?" Jaci asked him, her voice low and sexy. Ryan usually hated that question, thought it was such an invasion of his privacy, but this time, and with this woman, he didn't mind.

"I'm thinking that you are absolutely perfect and that I'm desperate to touch you, taste you." Ryan was surprised to hear the tremble in his voice. This was just sex, he reminded himself. He was just getting caught up in the moment, imagining more than what was actually there.

Except that Jaci was naked, open to his gaze, her face soft and her eyes blazing with desire. And trust. He could do anything right now, suggest anything, and she'd probably acquiesce. She was that into him and he was that crazy about her.

Jaci sat up and placed an openmouthed kiss on his lips. He put his hand on the back of her head to hold her there as her fingers went to the buttons on his black-and-white-checked shirt, ripping one or two off in her haste to get her hands on his skin. Then her small hands, cool and clever, pushed the shirt off his shoulders and danced across his skin, over his nipples, down his chest to tug on the waistband of his pants. Her mouth lifted off his and he felt bereft, wanting—no, needing—more.

"Need you naked." Jaci tugged on his pants again.

He summoned up enough willpower to resist her, wanting to keep her naked while he explored her body. He'd had a plan and that was to torture Jaci with his tongue and hands, kissing and loving those secret places and making her scream at least twice before he slid on home…

He shrugged out of his shirt and removed his socks and shoes, but his pants were staying on because discovering Jaci, pleasing Jaci, was more important than a quick orgasm. It took all of his willpower to grab her hand and pull it from his dick. He gently gripped her wrists and pushed them behind her back, holding them there while he dropped his head to suck a nipple into his mouth. From somewhere above him Jaci whimpered and arched her back, pushing her nipple against the roof of his mouth. Releasing her hands, he pushed her back and spent some time alternating between the two, licking and blowing and sucking.

He could make her come by just doing this, he realized, slightly awed. But he wanted more for her, from her. Leaving her breasts, he trailed his mouth across her ribs, down her stomach, probed her cute belly button with his tongue. He licked the path on each side of her landing strip and, feeling her tense, dipped between her folds and touched her, tasted her, circling her little nub with the tip of his tongue.

It all happened at once. He slid his finger inside her hot

channel, Jaci screamed, his tongue swirled in response and then she was pulsing and clenching around his fingers, thrusting her hips in a silent demand for more. He sucked again, pushed again and she arched her back and hips and shattered, again and again.

Ryan pulled out and dropped a kiss on her stomach before hand-walking his way up the bed to look into her feverish eyes. "Good?" he asked, balancing himself on one hand, biceps bulging, to push her hair out of her eyes.

"So good." Jaci linked her hands around his neck, her face flushed with pleasure and…yeah, awe.

He'd made her scream, he'd pushed her to heights he was pretty sure—judging by the dazed, surprised look on her face—that she hadn't felt before. Mission so accomplished.

Jaci's hands skimmed down his neck, down his sides to grip his hips, her thumbs skating over his obliques before she clasped him in both hands. He jerked and sighed and pushed himself into her hands. "Let me in," he begged. Begged! He'd never begged in his life.

"Nah." Jaci smiled that feminine smile that told him that he was in deep, deep trouble. The best type of trouble. "My turn to drive you crazy."

He knew that he was toast when, in the middle of fantastic, mind-altering sex he realized that this wasn't just sex. It was sex on steroids and that happened to him only when he became emotionally attached. Well, that had to stop, immediately. Well, maybe after she'd driven him crazy.

Maybe then.

Nine

Sunlight danced behind the blinds in Ryan's room as Jaci forced her eyes open the next morning. She was lying, as was her habit, on her stomach, limbs sprawled across the bed. And she was naked, which was not her habit. Jaci squinted across the wide expanse that was Ryan's chest and realized that her knee was nestled up against a very delicate part of his anatomy and that her arm was lying across his hips, his happy-to-see-you morning erection pressing into her skin.

She gazed at his profile and noticed that he looked a lot younger when his face was softened by sleep and a night of spectacular sex. Spectacular sex... Jaci pulled in a breath and closed her eyes as second and third and tenth thoughts slammed into her brain.

Why was she still lying in bed with him in a tangle of limbs and postorgasmic haze? She was smart enough to know that she should've taken the many orgasms he'd given her last night, politely said thank you and high-tailed it out of his apartment with a breezy smile and a "see you around." She shouldn't have allowed him to wrap his big arm around her waist or to haul her into a spooning position, her bottom perfectly nestled in his hips. She shouldn't have allowed herself to drift, sated and secure, feeling his nose in her hair, reveling in the soft kisses he placed on her shoulders, into her neck. She shouldn't have allowed herself the pleasure of fall-ing asleep in his arms.

Straight sex, uncomplicated sex, wham-bam sex she could handle; she knew what that was and how to deal with it. It was the optional extras that sent her into a spi-ral. The hand drifting over her hip, his foot caressing her calf, his thick biceps a pillow under her head. His easy affection scared the pants off her—well, they would if she were wearing any—and generated thoughts of *what if* and *I could get used to this*.

This wouldn't do, Jaci told herself, and gently—and reluctantly—removed her limbs from his body. Nothing had changed between them. They had just shared a physi-cal experience they'd both enjoyed. She was not going to get too anal about this. She wasn't going to overthink this. This was just sex, and it had nothing to do with the fact that they were boss and employee or even that they were becoming friends.

Sex was sex. Not to be confused with affection or car-ing or emotion or, God forbid, love. She'd learned that lesson and, by God, she'd learned it well. Jaci slipped out of bed, looking around for something to wear. Un-able to bear the thought of slipping into her dress from the night before—she'd be experiencing another walk of

shame through Ryan's apartment lobby soon enough—
she picked up his shirt from the night before and pulled
it over her head, grimacing as the cuffs fell a foot over
her hands. She was such a cliché, she thought, roughly
rolling back the fabric. The good girl in the bad boy's
bedroom, wearing his shirt...

After checking that Ryan was still asleep, Jaci rolled
her shoulders and looked around Ryan's room, taking in
the details she'd missed before. The bed, with its leather
headboard, dominated the room and complemented the
other two pieces of furniture: a black wing-back chair
and four-drawer credenza with a large mirror above it.
Jaci tipped her head as she noticed that there were photograph frames on the credenza but they were all facedown
and looked as if they'd been that way for a while. Curi-
ous, she padded across the room, past the half-open door
that led to a walk-in closet, and stood in front of the credenza. Her reflection in the mirror caused her to wince.
Her hair was a mess. She had flecks of mascara on her
eyelids, and on her jaw she could see red splotches from
Ryan rubbing his stubble-covered chin across her skin.
Her eyes were baggy and her face was pale with fatigue.

The morning after the night before, she thought,
rubbing her thumb over her eyes to remove the mascara. When the mascara refused to budge, she shrugged
and turned her attention back to the frames. Silver, she
thought, and a matching set. She lifted the first one up
and her breath caught in her throat as the golden image
of Ben, bubbling with life, grinned back at her. He looked
as if he was ready to step out of the frame, handsome and
sexy and so, well, alive. Hard to believe that he was gone,
Jaci thought. And if she found it hard, then his brother
would find it impossible, and she understood why Ryan

wouldn't want to be slapped in the face with the image of Ben, who was no more real than fairy dust.

And photograph number two? Jaci lifted up the frame and turned it over, then puzzled at the image of a dark-haired, dark-eyed woman who looked vaguely familiar. Who was this and why did she warrant being in an ornate, antique silver frame? She couldn't be Ryan's mother. This was a twenty-first-century woman through and through. Was she one of Ryan's previous lovers, possibly one who got away? But Ryan, according to the press, didn't have long-term relationships and she couldn't imagine that he'd keep a photo of a woman he'd had a brief affair with. Jaci felt the acid burn of jealously and wished she could will it away. You had to care about someone to be jealous and she didn't want to care about Ryan…not like that, anyway.

Jaci replaced the frame and when she looked at her reflection in the mirror, she saw that Ryan was standing behind her and that a curtain had fallen within his fabulous eyes. Her affectionate lover was gone.

"Don't bother asking," Ryan told her in a low, determined voice. He was as naked as a jaybird but his emotions were fully concealed. He might as well have been wearing a full suit of armor, Jaci thought. She couldn't help feeling hurt at his back-off expression; she found it so easy to talk to him but he, obviously, didn't feel the same.

Maybe she'd read this situation wrong; maybe they weren't even friends. Maybe the benefits they'd shared were exactly that, just benefits. The thought made her feel a little sad. And, surprisingly, deeply annoyed. How dare he make incredible, tender-but-hot love to her all night and then freeze her out before she'd even said good-morning?

The old Jaci, Lyon House Jaci, would just put her tail between her legs, scramble into her dress and apologize for upsetting him. New York Jaci had no intention of doing the same.

"That's it?" she demanded, hands on her hips. "That's all you're going to say?"

Ryan pushed a hand through his dark hair and Jaci couldn't miss his look of frustration. "I am not starting off the morning by having a discussion about her."

"Who is she?" Jaci demanded.

Ryan narrowed his eyes at her. "What part of 'not discussing this' didn't you hear?" He reached for a pair of jeans that draped across the back of his chair and pulled them on.

Jaci matched his frown with one of her own. "So it's okay for you to get me to spill my guts about my waste-of-space ex and his infidelities but you can't even open up enough to tell me who she is and why she's on your dresser?"

"Yes."

Jaci blinked at him.

"Yes, it's okay for you to do that and me not to," Ryan retorted. "I didn't torture you into telling me. It was your choice. Not telling you is mine."

Jaci pressed the ball of her hands to her temples. How had her almost perfect night morphed into something so… She wanted to say *ugly* but that wasn't the right word. Awkward? Unsettling? Uncomfortable? She desperately wanted to argue with him, to insist that they were friends, that he owed her an explanation, but she knew that he was right; it was his choice and he owed her nothing. He'd given her physical pleasure but there had been no promises to give her his trust, to let her breach his emotional walls. His past was his past, the girl in the photograph his business.

If his reluctance to talk, to confide in her, made her feel as if she was just another warm body for him to play with during the night, then that was her problem, not his. She would not be that demanding, insecure, irritating woman who'd push and pry and look to him to give more than he wanted to.

He'd wanted sex. He'd received sex and quite a lot of it. It had been fun, a physical release, and it was way past time for her to leave. Jaci dropped her eyes from his hard face, nodded quickly and managed to dredge up a cool smile and an even cooler tone. "Of course. Excuse me, I didn't mean to pry." She walked across the room, picked up her dress and her shoes, and gestured to the door to the en suite bathroom. "If I may?"

Ryan rubbed the back of his neck and sent her a hot look. "Don't use that snotty tone of voice with me. Just use the damn bathroom, Jace."

Hell, she just couldn't say the right thing this morning, Jaci thought. It was better if she just said nothing at all. Jaci walked toward the bathroom without looking at him again, silently cursing herself and calling herself all kinds of a fool.

Stupid, stupid, stupid. She should've left last night and avoided this morning-after-the-night-before awkwardness.

Lesson learned.

Stupid, stupid, stupid.

Ryan gripped the edge of the credenza with white-knuckled hands and straightened his arms, dropping his head to stare at the wooden floor beneath his bare feet. *You handled that with all the sophistication of a pot plant, moron.* She'd asked a simple question to which there was a simple answer.

Who is she?

There were many answers to that, some simple, some a great deal more complicated. *She was someone who was, once, important to me.* Or... *She was an ex-girlfriend.* Or that, *She was my fiancée.* Or, if he really wanted to stir up a hornets' nest, he could've said that she was Ben's lover.

All truth.

What a complete mess of the morning, Ryan thought, straightening. He stepped over to the window and yanked up the blind and looked down onto the greenery of Central Park in spring. It was a view he never failed to enjoy, but this morning he couldn't even do that, his thoughts too full of the woman—who was probably naked—in the next room.

Instead of slipping out of bed and getting dressed long before his lover woke up, this morning he'd opened his eyes on a cloud of contentment and had instinctively rolled over to pull her back into his arms. The empty space had been a shock to his system, a metaphorical bucket of icy water that instantly shriveled his morning erection. She'd left him, he'd thought, and the wave of disappointment that followed was even more of a shock. He did the leaving, he was in control, and the fact that he was scrambling to find his mental equilibrium floored him. He didn't like it.

At all.

He'd long ago perfected his morning-after routine, but nothing with Jaci was the same as those mindless, almost faceless encounters in his past. Last night had been the most intense sexual experience of his life to date and he hated that she'd had such an effect on him. He wanted to treat her like all those other encounters but he couldn't. She made him want things that he'd convinced himself he had no need for, things such as trust and comfort and support. She made him feel everything too intensely, made him question whether it was time to remove the barbed wire he'd wrapped his heart in.

Seeing her holding Kelly's photograph made him angry and, worse, confused. There was a damn good reason why he kept their photographs in a prominent place. Seeing them there every morning, even facedown, was like being flogged with a leather strap, but after the initial flash of pain, it was a good and solid reminder of why he chose to live his life the way he did. People couldn't be trusted; especially the people who were supposed to love you the most.

Yet a part of him insisted that Jaci was not another Kelly, that she'd never mangle his heart as she'd done, but then his common sense took over and reminded him that he couldn't take the chance. Love and trust—he'd never run the risk of having either of those emotions thrown back at him as if they meant nothing.

They meant something to him and he'd never risk them again.

It was better this way, Ryan told himself, sliding a glance toward the still-closed bathroom door. It was better that he and Jaci put some distance between them, allowed some time to dilute the crazy passion that swirled between them whenever they were alone. Because passion had a sneaky way of making you want more, tempting you to risk more than was healthy.

No, they needed that distance, and the sooner the better. Ryan walked into his closet, grabbed a T-shirt and shoved his feet into a pair of battered athletic shoes. He raked his hands through his hair, walked back into his bedroom and picked up his wallet from the credenza, in front of the now-upright photo of Ben.

"Hey, Jaci?" Ryan waited for her response before speaking again in an almost jovial voice. God, the last thing in the world he felt was jovial. He felt horny, and frustrated and a little sick, but not jovial. "I'm running out for bagels and coffee. I'll be back in ten."

He already knew how she'd respond and she didn't disappoint. "I won't be here when you get back. I've got a…thing."

She didn't have a thing any more than he wanted bagels and coffee but it was an out and he'd take it. "Okay. Later."

Later? Ryan saw that his hand was heading for the doorknob and he ruthlessly jerked it back. He was not going in there. If he saw Jaci again he'd want to take her to bed and that would lead to more confusing…well, feelings, and he didn't need this touchy-feely crap.

Keep telling yourself that, Jackson. Maybe you'll start to believe it sometime soon.

It was spring and the sprawling gardens at Lyon House, Shropshire, had never looked so beautiful with beds of daffodils and bluebells nodding in the temperate breeze. At the far edge of the lawn, behind the wedding tent, it looked as if a gardener had taken a sponge and dabbed the landscape with colored splotches of rhododendron and azalea bushes, a mishmash of brilliant color that hurt the eyes.

It was beautiful, it was home.

And she was miserable.

Sitting in the chapel that had stood for centuries ad-
jacent to Lyon House, Jaci rolled her head to work out
the kinks in her neck. If she looked out the tiny window
to her left, she could see the copse of trees that sepa-
rated the house from the chapel, and beyond that the
enormous white designer fairy-tale tent—with its own
dance floor—that occupied most of the back lawn. It
was fairly close to what she'd planned for her own wedding, which had been scheduled for six weeks from now.
Like the bride, she would've dressed at Lyon House, in
her old room, and her mother would've bossed everyone
about as she had been doing all day. The grounds would
have been as spectacular, and she would've had as many
guests. Like Neil, her groom would've been expectant,
nervous, excited.

Her only thought about her canceled wedding was that
she'd dodged a bullet. And then she'd run to the States,
where she'd fallen into the flight path of a freakin' ba-
zooka. Jaci blew her frustration out and sneaked another
look at Ryan. So far she'd spent a lot of the ceremony
admiring his broad shoulders, tight butt and long legs,
and remembering what he looked like naked. Jaci wig-
gled in her seat, realizing that it was very inappropriate
to be thinking of a naked man in a sixteenth-century
English church. Or, come to think of it, *any* church, for
that matter...

Jaci crossed her legs and thought that she should be
used to seeing him in a tuxedo, but today he looked better than he had any right to. The ice-blue tie turned his
eyes the same color and she noticed that he'd recently
had his hair trimmed. He'd spent the week avoiding her

since their—what could she call it?—*encounter* in LA, and while her brain thought that some time apart was a wonderful idea, every other organ she possessed missed him. To a ridiculous degree. She sighed and sent another longing look at his profile. So sexy, and when he snapped his head around and caught her looking, she flushed.

No phone call. No email. No text. Nothing, she reminded herself. It was horrifying to realize that if he so much as crooked his baby finger she'd kick off her shoes, scramble over the seats and, bridal couple be damned, fly into his arms.

She wanted him. She didn't want to want him.

A slim arm wrapping around her waist had her turning, and she sighed at the familiar perfume. Meredith, her big sister, with her jet-black, geometric bob, red lipstick and almost oriental eyes looked sharp and sleekly sexy in a black sheath that looked as if it had been painted on her skinny frame. Twelve-year-olds had thighs fatter than hers, Jaci thought.

Merry gave her shoulders a squeeze. "Hey, are you okay?"

Jaci lifted one shoulder. How should she answer that? *No, my life is an even bigger mess now than it was when I left. I might not have a job soon and I think I might be in love with my fake boyfriend, who has the communication skills of a clam. That's the same fake boyfriend who left New York the morning after a night of marvelous sex. The same one whom I haven't spoken to or had an email or a text or a smoke signal from.*

Not that she was sure she wanted to talk to the moronic, standoffish, distant man who used a stupid excuse to run out of his apartment as quickly as he could. As if he could fool her with that bagels-and-coffee comment.

After Clive she had a master's degree in the subject of crap-men-say.

Merry spoke in her ear. "So…you and Ryan."

"There is no me and Ryan," Jaci retorted, her voice a low whisper.

Merry looked at Ryan and licked her lips. "He is a *babe*, I have to admit. Mum thinks you're having a thing."

"The supposed relationship between us has been wildly exaggerated." Nobody could call a few hot nights a relationship, could they?

"Come on, tell me." Meredith jammed an elbow in her ribs.

The elderly aunt on her other side nudged her in the ribs. "Shh! The reverend is trying to give his sermon!"

"And I'm trying not to fall asleep." Merry yawned.

Ryan shifted his position and subtly turned so that he was practically facing her and she felt his eyes, like gentle fingers, trace her features, skim her cheekbones, her lower lips, down to her mouth. When his eyes dropped to look at her chest, her nipples responded by puckering against the fabric of her dress. The corners of Ryan's mouth lifted in response and she flamed again. Traitorous body, she silently cursed, folding her arms across her chest and narrowing her eyes.

"Some of your attention should be on your brother," Merry said out of the side of her mouth. "You know, the guy who is getting married to the girl in the white dress?"

"Can't help it, he drives me batty," Jaci replied, sotto voce. "He's arrogant and annoying and…annoying. The situation between us is…complicated."

"Complicated or not he is, holy bananas, *so* sexy."

Priscilla, on the bench in front of them, spun around in her seat and sent them her evil-mother laser glare. Her purple fascinator bounced and she slapped a feather out of her eye. Her voice, slightly quieter than a foghorn, boomed through the church. "Will you two please be quiet or must I put you outside?"

If Jaci hadn't been so embarrassed she might have been amused to see her ever-cool and unflappable world-class-journalist sister slide down in her seat and place her hand over her eyes.

Ten

The band was playing those long, slow songs that bands played for the diehard guests who couldn't tear themselves away from the free booze or the dance floor or, as was Merry's case, the company of a cousin of the bride. Her sister looked animated and excited, Jaci thought, watching them from her seat at a corner table, now deserted. She hoped that the man wasn't married or gay or a jerk. Her sister deserved to have some fun, deserved a good man in her life. Always so serious and so driven, it would be good for her to have someone in her life who provided her with some balance. And some hot sex. You couldn't go wrong with some hot sex.

Well, you could if you were on the precipice of falling in love with the man who, up to a couple of days ago, had provided you with some very excellent sex. Jaci closed her eyes and rested her temple against her fist. She couldn't be that stupid to be falling in love with Ryan, could she? Maybe she was just confusing liking with love. Maybe she was confused because he made her feel so amazing in bed.

If so, why did she miss him so intensely when he wasn't with her? Why did she think about him constantly? Why did she wish that she could provide him with the emotional support he gave to her by just standing at her side and breathing? Why did she want to make his life better, brighter, happier? She couldn't blame that on sexual attraction or even on friendship.

Nope, she was on the verge of yanking her heart out and handing it over to him. And if she did that, she knew that if he refused to take it, which he would because Ryan didn't do commitment in any shape or form, it would be forever mangled and never quite the same. She had to pull back, had to protect herself. Hadn't her heart and her confidence and her psyche endured enough of a battering lately? Why would she want to torture herself some more?

A strong, tanned hand placed a cup full of hot coffee in front of her and she looked up into Ryan's eyes. "You look like you need that," he said, taking the chair next to her and flipping it so that he faced her, his long legs stretched out in front of him.

"Thanks. I thought you were avoiding me."

"Trying to." Ryan sent her a brooding look before looking at his watch. "I managed it for six hours but I'm caving."

Jaci lifted her eyebrows. "That's eight days and six hours. I heard you went to LA."

Ryan glowered at her. "Yeah. Waste of a trip since I spent most of my time thinking of you. Naked."

Lust, desire, need swirled between them. How was she supposed to respond to that? Should she tell him that she'd spent less time writing and more time fantasizing? *He's still your boss*, she reminded herself. Maybe she should keep that to herself.

"I've spent most of the evening watching you talk to your ex." Ryan frowned.

Now, that was an exaggeration. She'd spoken to Clive, sure, but not for that long and not for the whole evening.

"You're not seriously considering giving him another chance, are you?" Ryan demanded, his eyes and voice hot.

No calls, no text messages, no emails and now stupid questions. Jaci sighed. Going back to Clive after being with Ryan would be like living in a tiny tent after occupying a mansion. In other words, completely horrible. But because he'd been such a moron lately, she was disinclined to give him the assurance his question seemed to demand. Or was she just imagining the thread of concern she heard in his voice?

That was highly possible.

"Talk to me, Jace," Ryan said when she didn't answer him.

Jaci's lips pressed together. "You're joking, right? Do you honestly think that you can sleep with me and then freeze me out when I ask a personal question? Do you really think it's okay for you not to call me, to avoid me for the best part of a week?"

Ryan released a curse and rubbed the back of his neck. "I'm sorry about that."

Jaci didn't buy his apology. "Sure you are. But I bet that if I suggest that we go back to your B and B you'd be all over that idea."

"Of course I would be. I'm a man and you're the best sex I've ever had." Jaci widened her eyes at his statement. The best sex? Ever? *Really?*

"Dammit, Jace, you tie me up in knots." Ryan tipped his head back to look at the ceiling of the tent. The main lights had been turned out and only flickering fairy lights illuminated the tent, casting dancing shadows on his tired face. What was she supposed to say to that? *Sorry that I've complicated your life? Sorry that I'm the best sex you've ever had?*

She'd apologized for too many things in her life, many of them that weren't her fault, but she would be damned if she was going to apologize to Ryan. Not about this. She liked the fact that she, at least, had some effect on the man. So Jaci just crossed her legs and didn't bother to adjust her dress when the fabric parted and exposed her knee and a good portion of her thigh. She watched Ryan's eyes drop to her legs, saw the tension that skittered through his body and the way his Adam's apple bobbed in his throat.

Another knot, she thought. Good, let him feel all crazy for a change.

Instead of touching her as she expected, Ryan sat up, took a sip of her coffee and, after putting her cup back in its saucer, tapped his finger on the white damask tablecloth. "I'm not good at sharing my thoughts, at talking."

That didn't warrant a response, so Jaci just looked at him.

"I have a messed-up relationship with my family, both dead and alive." Ryan stared off into the distance. "My mother is dead, my father is a stranger to me, someone who always put his needs above those of his kids. I'm not looking for sympathy, I'm just telling you how it was."

Ryan stopped talking and hauled in another breath. It took a moment for his words to sink in, to realize that he was talking to her. Jaci's heart stopped momentarily and then it started to pound. He was *talking* to her? For real?

"I don't talk to people because I don't want them getting that deep into my head," Ryan admitted with a lot of reluctance. He closed his eyes momentarily before speaking again. "That girl in the picture? Well, she died in the same car accident as Ben."

"Ben's fiancée? I'm sorry but I don't remember her name." And why did he have a photograph of Ben's fiancée in his bedroom? Facedown, but still…

"Kelly. Everyone thought that she was engaged to Ben because she was wearing an engagement ring," Ryan said, but something in his voice had Jaci leaning forward, trying to look into his eyes. Judging by his hard expression, and by the muscle jumping in his cheek, talking about Ben and this woman was intensely difficult for Ryan. Of course, they were talking about his brother's death. It had to be hard, but there was more to this story than she was aware of.

Ryan stared at the ground between his knees and pulled in a huge breath, and Jaci was quite sure that he wasn't aware that his hand moved across the table to link with hers. "Kelly wasn't Ben's fiancée, she was mine."

Jaci tangled her fingers in his and held on. "What?"

Ryan lifted his head and dredged up a smile but his eyes remained bleak. "Yeah, we'd got engaged two weeks earlier."

Jaci struggled to make sense of what he was saying. "But the press confirmed that they had spent a romantic weekend together." Jaci swore softly when she realized what he was trying to tell her. "She was *cheating.*

On you." She lifted her hand to her mouth, aghast. "Oh, Ryan!"

How horrible was that? Jaci felt her stomach bubble, felt the bile in the back of her throat. His fiancée and his brother were having an affair and he found out when they both died in a car crash? That was like pouring nitric acid into a throat wound. How…how…how dare they?

How did anyone deal with that, deal with losing two people you loved and finding out they were having an affair behind your back? What were you supposed to feel? Do? Act? God, no wonder Ryan had such massive trust issues.

Fury followed horror. Who slept with her fiancé's brother, who slept with their brother's fiancée? *Who did that?* She was so angry she could spit radioactive spiders. "I am so mad right now," was all she could say.

The corners of Ryan's mouth lifted and his eyes lightened a fraction. "It was a long time ago, honey." He removed his fingers from her grasp and flexed his hand. "Ow."

"Sorry, but that disloyalty, that amount of selfishness—"

Ryan placed the tips of his fingers on her mouth to stop her talking. Jaci sighed and yanked her words back. It didn't matter how angry she was on his behalf, how protective she was feeling, the last thing he needed was for her to go all psycho on him. Especially since Ben and Kelly had paid the ultimate price.

"Sorry, Ry," she muttered around his fingers.

"Yeah. Me, too." Ryan dropped his hand. "I never talk about it—nobody but me knows. Kelly wanted to keep the engagement secret—"

"Probably because she was boinking your brother."

"Thank you, I hadn't realized that myself," Ryan said, his voice bone-dry.

Jaci winced. "Sorry." It seemed as if it was her go-to phrase tonight.

"Anyway, you're the first person I've told. Ever." Ryan shoved his hand through his hair. "You asked who she was and I wanted to tell you, but I *didn't* want to tell you and it all just got too…"

Jaci waited a beat before suggesting a word. "Real?"

Ryan nodded. "Yeah. If I explained, I couldn't keep pretending that we were just…friends."

What did that mean? Were they more than friends now? Was he also feeling something deeper than passion and attraction, something that could blossom and grow into…something deeper? Jaci wished she had the guts to ask him, but a part of her didn't want to risk hearing his answer. It might not be what she was looking for or even wanting. Her heart was in her hands and she was mentally begging him to take it, to keep it. But she wanted him to keep it safe and she wasn't sure that he would.

Ryan closed his eyes and rubbed his eyelids with his thumb and forefinger. "God, I'm tired."

"Then go back to the B and B," Jaci suggested.

"Will you come with me?"

Jaci cocked her head in thought. She could but if she did she knew that she would have no more defenses against him, that she would give him everything she had, and she knew that she couldn't afford to do that. And, despite the fact that he'd opened up, he wasn't anywhere near being in love with her and he didn't want what she did. Oh, she was in love with him. He had most of her heart, but she was keeping a little piece of that organ back, and all of her soul, because she needed them to carry on, to survive when he left.

Because he would leave. This was her life, not a fairy tale.

He stood up and held out his hand. "Jace? You coming?"

"Sorry, Ry."

Ryan frowned at her and looked across the room to where Clive stood, watching them. Watching *her.* Creepy. "You've got something better to do?" Ryan demanded, his eyes dark with jealously.

"Oh, Ryan, you are such an idiot!" she murmured.

She was tempted to go with him, of course she was. Despite his opening up and letting her a little way in, they weren't in a committed relationship, and the more she slept with him the deeper in love she would fall. She had to be sensible, had to keep some distance. But she didn't want to make light of the fact that he'd confided in her and that she appreciated his gesture, so Jaci reached up and touched her lips to his cheek. Then she held her cheek against his, keeping her eyes closed as she inhaled his intoxicating smell. "Thank you for telling me, Ry."

The tips of Ryan's fingers dug into her hips. He rested his forehead on hers and sighed heavily. "You drive me nuts."

Jaci allowed a small laugh to escape. "Right back at you, bud. Are you coming to the family breakfast in the morning?"

"Yeah." Ryan kissed her nose before stepping back. He tossed a warning glance in Clive's direction. "Don't let him snow you, Jace. He's a politician and by all reports he's a good one."

"So?"

"So, don't let him con you," Ryan replied impatiently. "He cheated on you and lied to you and treated you badly. Don't get sucked back in."

Jaci looked at him, astounded. She wasn't a child and she wasn't an idiot and she knew, better than anybody, what a jerk Clive was. Did she come across that naive, that silly, that in need of protection? She was a grown woman and she knew her own mind. She wasn't the weak-willed, wafty, soft person Ryan and her family saw her as. Sometimes she wondered if anyone would ever notice that she'd grown up, that she was bigger, stronger, bolder. Would they ever see her as she was now? Would anyone ever really know her?

She didn't need a prince or a knight to run to her rescue anymore.

She'd slay her own dragons, thank you very much, and she'd look after herself while she did it.

The next morning Jaci, her mother and Merry sat on the terrace and watched as the people from the catering company dismantled the tent and cleared up the wedding detritus. When Ryan got there they would haul Archie out of his study and they'd rustle up some breakfast. The bride and groom would arrive when they did—they weren't going to wait for them—but for now she was happy to sit on the terrace in the spring sunshine.

"One down, two to go," Priscilla stated without looking up. Her mother, wearing an enormous floppy hat, sat next to her, a rough draft of her newest manuscript in her hands.

"Don't look at me," Merry categorically stated, placing her bare feet on the arm of Jaci's chair.

"It should've been my marriage next," Jaci quietly stated.

"Speaking of," Merry said, "I saw you talking to Clive last night. You looked very civilized. Why weren't you slapping his face and scratching his eyes out?"

Jaci rested her cup of coffee on her knee. "Because I don't care about him anymore. He's coming here today. I stored some things of his in my room that he needs to collect." Jaci pushed her sunglasses up her nose. "Once that's done I'll be free of him, forever."

Merry snorted her disbelief and Jaci wanted to tell her that it was true because she was in love with Ryan, but that was too new, too precious to share.

"So what did you talk about?" Merry asked. "Your relationship?"

"A little. He was very apologetic and sweet about it. He groveled a bit and that was nice."

"I don't buy it," Merry stated, her eyes narrowed. "Clive isn't the type to grovel."

Merry was so damn cynical sometimes, Jaci thought. "Look, he tried to talk me into trying again but I told him about New York, about everything that happened there and how happy I was. He eventually gave up and said that he understood. He wished me well and we parted on good terms."

"Clive doesn't like hearing the word *no*," Merry stated, her lips in a thin line. "I don't trust him. Be careful of him."

Merry really was overreacting, thought Jaci, bored with talking about her ex.

"And Ryan?" Merry asked.

Ryan? Jaci rested her head on the back of her chair. "I don't know, Merry. He has his own issues to work through.

I don't know if we will ever be anything more than just friends."

"He doesn't look at you like you're just friends," Merry said.

"That's just because we are really good in bed together," Jaci retorted, and sent her mother a guilty look. "Sorry, Mum."

"I know you had sex with him, child," Priscilla drily replied. "I'm not that much of a prude or that oblivious. I have had, and for your information, still do have, a sex life."

"God." Jaci placed her hand over her eyes and Merry groaned. "Thanks for putting that thought into my head. Eeew. Anyway, coming back to Ryan…he's a closed book in so many ways. I take one step forward with him and sixty back. I thought we took a couple of steps forward last night."

"I thought you said that things are casual between you," Merry said.

"They are." Jaci tugged at the ragged hem of her denim shorts. "Sort of. As I said, I think we turned a corner last night but, knowing me, I might be reading the situation wrong." She pulled her earlobe. "I tend to do that with men. I'm pretty stupid when it comes to relationships."

"We all are, in one way or another," Merry told her.

"Yeah, but I tend to take stupidity to new heights," Jaci replied, tipping her face up to the sun. She'd kissed Ryan impulsively, agreed to be his pretend girlfriend, slept with him and then fell in love with him. *Stupid* didn't even begin to cover it.

Well, she'd made those choices and now she had to live the consequences…

Jaci jerked when she heard the slap of paper hitting

the stone floor and she winced when the wind picked up her mother's manuscript and blew sheets across the terrace. Before her mother could get hysterical about losing her work, Jaci jumped up to retrieve the pages, but Priscilla's whip-crack voice stopped her instantly. "Sit down, Jacqueline!"

"But...your papers." Jaci protested.

"Leave them," Priscilla ordered and Jaci frowned. Who was this person and what had she done with her mother? The Priscilla Jaci knew would be having six kittens and a couple of ducks by now at the thought of losing her work.

Priscilla yanked off her hat and shoved her hand into her short cap of gray hair. She frowned at Jaci but her eyes looked sad. "I don't ever want to hear those words out of your mouth again."

Jaci quickly tried to recall what she'd said and couldn't pinpoint the source of her ire. "What words?"

"That you are stupid. I won't have it, do you understand?"

Jaci felt as if she was being sucked into a parallel universe where nothing made sense. Before she could speak, Priscilla held up her hand and shook her head. "You are not stupid, do you understand me?" Priscilla stated, her voice trembling with emotion. "You are more intelligent than the rest of us put together!"

No, she wasn't. "Mum—"

"None of us could have coped with what Clive put you through with the grace and dignity you did. We just shoved our heads in the sand and ignored him, hoping that he would go away. But you had to deal with him, with the press. The four of us deal with life by ignoring what makes us unhappy and we're selfish, horrible creatures."

"It's okay, Mum. *I'm* okay."

Jaci flicked a look at Merry, who appeared equally uncomfortable at their mother's statement. "It's not okay. It's not okay that you've spent your life believing that you are second-rate because you are not obsessive and self-ish and driven and ambitious."

"But I'm not smart like you." Jaci stared at her inter-twined fingers.

"No, but you're smart like you," Merry quietly said. "Instead of falling apart when Clive raked you, and your relationship, through the press, you picked yourself up, dusted yourself off and started something new. You pur-sued your dream and got a job and you started a new life, and that takes guts, kid. Mum's right. We ignore what we don't understand and bury ourselves, and our emo-tions, in our work."

Jaci let out a low, trembling laugh. "Let's not get too carried away. I'm a scriptwriter. It's not exactly *War and Peace*."

"It's a craft," Priscilla insisted. "A craft that you seem to excel at, as I've recently realized. I'm sorry that you felt like you couldn't share that with us, that you thought that we wouldn't support you. God, I'm a terrible mother. I'm the failure, Jaci, not you. You are, by far, the best of us."

Merry reached out and squeezed her shoulder. "I'm sorry, too, Jace. I haven't exactly been there for you."

Jaci blinked away the tears in her eyes and swallowed the lump in her throat. What a weekend this had been, she thought; she'd fallen in love and she'd realized that she was a part of the Brookes-Lyon family—quite an im-portant part, as it turned out. She was the normal one. The rest of her family were all slightly touched. Clever but a bit batty.

It was, she had to admit, a huge relief.

"And you are not stupid when it comes to men," Priscilla stated, her voice now strong and back to its normal no-nonsense tone. "Ryan is thick if he can't see how wonderful you are."

She wished she could tell them about Ben and Kelly's betrayal, but that was Ryan's story, not hers. Maybe they had made some progress last night, but how much? Jaci knew that Ryan wasn't the type to throw caution to the wind and tumble into a relationship with her; he might have told her the reasons for his wariness and reserve but he hadn't told her that he had any plans to change his mind about trusting, about loving someone new. She knew that he would still be the same guarded, restrained, unable-to-trust person he currently was, and she didn't know if she could live with that…long term. How did you prove yourself worthy of someone's trust, someone's love? And if she ignored these concerns and they fell back into bed, she'd be happy until the next time he emotionally, or physically, disappeared. And she would be hurt all over again. She could see the pattern evolving before her eyes, and she didn't want to play that game.

She wanted a relationship, she wanted love, she wanted forever.

Jaci gnawed at her bottom lip. "I don't know where I stand with him."

Priscilla sent her a steady look. "As much as I like Ryan, if you can't work that out, and if he won't tell you, then maybe it's time that you stopped standing and started walking."

Stop standing and start walking… Jaci felt the truth of her mum's words lodge in her soul. Would Ryan ever let her be, well, more? Was she willing to stand around waiting for him to make up his mind? Was she willing to try to prove herself worthy of his love? His trust?

But did she have the strength to let him go? She didn't think so. Maybe the solution was to give him a little time to get used to having someone in his life again. After all that he'd suffered, was that such a big ask? In a month—or two or three—she could reevaluate, see whether he'd made any progress in the trust department. That was fair, wasn't it?

Jaci had the niggling thought that she was conning herself, that she was delaying the inevitable, but when she heard the sound of a car pulling up outside she pushed out her doubts and jumped to her feet, a huge smile blossoming.

"He's here!" she squealed, running to the edge of the railing and leaning over to catch a glimpse of the car rolling up the drive. Her face fell when she recognized Clive's vintage Jaguar. She pouted. "Damn, it's Clive."

Merry caught Priscilla's eye. "Music to my ears," she said, sotto voce.

Priscilla smiled and nodded. "Mine, too."

Eleven

Ryan, parking his rental car in the driveway of Lyon House, felt as if he had a rope around his neck and barbed wire around his heart. He looked up at the ivy-covered, butter-colored stone house and wondered which window on the second floor was Jaci's bedroom. The one with frothy white curtains blowing in the breeze? It would have been, he thought, a lot easier if they'd spent the night having sex instead of talking. Sex, that physical connection, he knew how to deal with, but talking, exposing himself? Not so much.

If he wanted to snow himself, he supposed he could try to convince himself that he'd told her about Ben and Kelly's deception, their betrayal, as a quid pro quo for her telling him about her disastrous engagement to Horse-face. But he'd had many women bawl on his shoulder while they told him their woes and he'd never felt the need to return the favor.

Jaci, unfortunately, could not be lumped into the masses.

Ryan leaned his head against the headrest and closed his eyes. What a week. In his effort to treat her like a flash-in-the-pan affair, he'd kept his distance by putting the continent between them, but he'd just made himself miserable. He'd missed her. Intensely. His work and the drive and energy he gave it made his career his primary focus, but he'd had only half his brain on business this past week. Not clever when so much was at stake.

He had to make a decision about what to do with her, about her, soon. He knew that she wasn't the type to have a no-strings affair. Her entire nature was geared to being in a steady relationship, to being committed and cared for. She was paying lip service to the idea of a fling but sooner or later her feelings would run deeper... His might, too.

He'd put his feelings away four years ago, and he didn't like the fact that Jaci had the ability to make him feel more, be more, made him want to be the best version of himself, for her. She was becoming too important and if he was going to walk, if he was going to keep his life emotionally uncomplicated, then he had to walk away *now*. He couldn't sleep with her again because every time they had sex, every moment he had with her, with every word she spoke, she burrowed further under his skin. He had to act because his middle ground was fast disappearing.

Ryan picked up his wallet and mobile from the console and opened his door on a large sigh. It was so much easier to remain single, he thought. His life had been so uncomplicated before Jaci.

Boring, admittedly, but uncomplicated. Ryan turned to close the car door and saw Jaci's father turning the corner to walk up the steps. "Morning, Archie," he said, holding out his hand for Jaci's father to shake. "Have you seen Jaci?"

Archie, vague about anything that didn't concern his newspaper or world news, thought for a moment. "In her room, with the politician," he eventually said.

Blood roared through Ryan's head. "Say what?" he said, sounding as if he was being strangled. What the hell did that mean? Had Whips and Chains spent the night? With Jaci?

What the…

"Ryan!"

Ryan looked up as Jaci's slim figure walked out of the front door of Lyon House, her ex close on her heels. He had a duffel bag slung over his shoulder and his hand on Jaci's back, and he sent Ryan a look that screamed *Yeah, I did her and it was fantastic, dude.* Ryan clenched his fist as Jaci skipped down the stairs. He could watch her forever, he thought, as she approached him with a smile on her face that lit her from the inside out. God, she was beautiful, he thought. Funny, smart, dedicated. Confident, sexy and, finally, starting to realize who she was and her place in the world.

Clive greeted Archie as he walked back into the house, then he kissed Jaci's cheek, told her to give him a call and walked toward his car. Jaci stared at Clive's departing back for more time than Ryan was comfortable with and when she turned to look at him she was—damn, what was the word?—*glowing.* She looked—the realization felt like a fist slamming into his stomach—soft and radiant, the way she looked after they'd shared confidences, exactly the way she looked after they made love. Her eyes were a gooey brown, filled with emotion. He could read hope there and possibilities and…love. He saw love.

Except that *they* hadn't made love. He hadn't made love…

Jesus, no.

Maybe she *had* slept with Whips and Chains again, Ryan thought, his mind accelerating to the red zone. It was highly possible; three months ago she'd loved him, was planning to marry him. Those feelings didn't just disappear, evaporate. He was a politician and he probably talked her around and charmed her back into bed. Had he read too much into whatever he and Jaci had? Had it just been a sexual fling? Maybe, possibly…after all, Jaci hadn't given him the slightest indication of her desire to deepen this relationship, so was he rolling the wrong credits? They'd slept together a couple of times. For all he knew, she might just regard him as a way to pass some time until her ex came to his senses.

Did Jaci still love Clive? The idea wasn't crazy; yeah, the guy was a jerk-nugget, but love didn't just go away. God, he still loved Ben despite the fact that he'd betrayed him, and a part of him still loved Kelly, even after five years and everything that happened.

But, God, it stung like acid to think of Jaci and Clive in bed, that moron touching her perfect body, pulling her back into his life. He'd shared a woman before and he would *never* do it again. Ryan felt the bile rise up in his throat and he ruthlessly choked it down. God, he couldn't be sick, not now.

Feeling sideswiped, he looked down and noticed that his mobile, set to silent, was ringing. He frowned at the unfamiliar number on the screen. Thinking that taking the call would give him some time to corral his crazy thoughts, he pushed the green button and lifted the phone to his ear.

"Jax? This is Jet Simons."

Ryan's frown deepened. Why would Simons, the slimiest tabloid writer around, be calling him and how the hell did he get his number? He considered disconnecting, blowing him off, but maybe there was a fire he needed to put out. "What the hell do you want? And how did you get my number?"

"I have my sources. So, I hear that you and Jaci Brookes-Lyon think that Leroy Banks is a slimy troll and that you two are pretending to be in a relationship to keep him sweet. What did you two call him, 'Toad of Toad Hall'?"

Ryan's eyes flew to Jaci's face. The harsh swear left his mouth, and only after it was out did he realize that it, in itself, was the confirmation Simons needed.

"No comment," he growled, wishing he could reach through the phone and wrap his hand around Simons's scrawny neck. Strangling Jaci was an option, too. She was the only person who used that expression. He sent her a dark look and she instinctively took a step back.

"So is that a yes?" Simons persisted.

"It's a 'no comment.' Who did you get that story from?" Ryan rested his fist against his forehead.

Simons laughed. "I had a trans-Atlantic call earlier. Tell Jaci that you can never trust a politician."

"Egglestone is your source?" Ryan demanded, and Simons's silence was enough of an answer.

Yep, it seemed that Jaci had shared quite a bit during their pillow talk. Ryan sent her another blistering look, deliberately ignoring her pleading, confused face. Ryan felt the hard, cold knot of despair and anger settle like a concrete brick in his stomach. He remembered this feeling. He'd lived with it for months, years after Ben and Kelly died. God, he wanted to punch something. Preferably Simons.

He was furiously angry and he needed to stay that way. This was why he didn't get involved in relationships; it was bad enough that his heart was in a mess and his love life was chaotic. Now it was affecting his business. Where had this gone so damn wrong?

He hated to ask Simons a damn thing, but he needed to know how much time he had before he took a trip up that creek without a paddle. "When are you running the story?"

"Can't," Simons said cheerfully. "Banks threatened to sue the hell out of my paper if we so much as mentioned his name and my editor killed it. That's why I feel nothing about giving up my source."

"You spoke to Banks?" Ryan demanded. He felt a scream starting to build inside him. This was it, this was the end. His business had been pushed backward and Jaci's career was all but blown out of the water.

"Yeah, he was...um, what's the word? *Livid*?" Ryan could hear the smile in his voice. The jackass was enjoying every second of this. "He told me to tell you to take your movie and shove it—"

"Got it." Ryan interrupted him. "So, basically, you just called me to screw with me?"

"Basically," Simons agreed.

Ryan told him to do something physically impossible and disconnected the call. He tossed his mobile through the open window of the car onto the passenger seat and linked his hands behind his neck.

"What's happened?" Jaci asked, obviously worried.

"That must have been a hell of a cozy conversation you had with Horse-face last night. It sounds like you covered a hell of a lot of ground."

Jaci frowned. "I don't understand."

"Your pillow talk torpedoed any chance of Banks funding *Blown Away*," he stated in his harshest voice.

Jaci looked puzzled. "What pillow talk? What are you talking about? Has Banks pulled his funding?" Jaci demanded, looking surprised.

"Your boyfriend called Simons and told him the whole story about how we snowed Banks, how we pretended to be a couple because he repulsed you. Nice job, kid. Thanks for that. The movie is dead and so is your career." He knew that he should shut up but he was so hurt, so angry, and he needed to hurt her, needed her to be in as much pain as he was. He just wished he was as angry at losing the funding as he was at the idea of Jaci sleeping with that slimy politician. Of losing Jaci to him.

Jaci just stood in the driveway and stared at him, her dark eyes filled with an emotion he couldn't identify. "Are you crazy?" she whispered.

"Crazy for thinking you could be trusted." Ryan tossed the statement over his shoulder as he yanked open the door to the car and climbed inside. "I should've run as hard and as fast as I could right after you kissed me. You've been nothing but a hassle. You've caused so much drama in my life I doubt I'll ever dig myself out of it. You know, you're right. You are the Brookes-Lyon screwup!"

Ryan watched as the poison-tipped words struck her soul, and he had to grab the steering wheel to keep from bailing out of the car and whisking her into his arms as she shrunk in on herself. He loved her, but he wanted to hurt her. He didn't understand it and he wasn't proud of it, but it was true. Because, unlike four years ago, this time he could fight back.

This time he could, verbally, punch and kick. He could retaliate and he wouldn't have to spend the rest of his life resenting the fact that death had robbed him of his chance to confront those who'd hurt him. He could hurt back and it felt—dammit—good!

"Why are you acting like this? Yes, I told Clive about Banks, about New York, but I never thought that he would blab to the press! I thought that we were friends again, that we had come to an understanding last night."

"Yet you still hopped into bed with that horse's ass."

"I did not sleep with Clive!" Jaci shouted.

Sure, you didn't, he mentally scoffed. Ryan started the engine of the car. He stared at the gearshift before jamming it into Reverse. He backed up quickly and pushed the button to take down the window of the passenger door. On the other side of the car stood Jaci, tears running down her face. He couldn't let her desperate, confused, emotional expression affect him. He wouldn't let anything affect him again…not when it came to her, or any other woman, either.

He didn't trust those tears, didn't trust her devastated expression. He didn't trust her. At all. "Thanks for screwing up my life, honey. I owe you one."

"Have you been fired?" Shona asked, perching her bottom on the corner of the desk Jaci was emptying.

It was Wednesday. Jaci'd been back in New York for two days and she'd sent Ryan two emails and left three voice mails asking him to talk to her and hadn't received a reply. Ryan, she concluded, was ignoring her.

She'd reached out five times and he'd ignored her five times. Yeah, she got the message.

"Resigned. I'm saving them the hassle of letting me go," Jaci said, tossing her thesaurus into her tote bag. "Without funding, *Blown Away* is dead in the water and I'm not needed."

Shona tapped her fingernails on her desk in a rat-a-tat-tat that set Jaci's teeth on edge. "I hear that Jax has been in meetings from daybreak to midnight trying to get other funding."

Jaci wasn't one to put any stock in office rumors. No, Ryan had moved on. It was that simple.

Thanks for screwing up my life, honey...

Moron man! How *dare* he think that she'd slept with Clive? Yes, she told Clive about Leroy, but only because a part of her wanted him to see that she was happy and content without him, that she had other men in her life and that she wasn't pining for him. But she'd forgotten that Clive hated to share and that he still, despite everything, considered her his. Under those genial smiles was a man who had still been hell-bent on punishing her; payback for the fact that she'd had the temerity to move on to Ryan from him. But while she knew that Clive could be petty, she'd never thought that he'd be so vengeful, so malicious as to call up a tabloid reporter and cause so much trouble for her and Ryan.

Oh, she was so mad. How dare Ryan have so little faith in her? How could he think that she would sleep with someone else, and just after they'd shared something so deep, as important as they had earlier that night? She might have a loose mouth and trust people too easily and believe that they were better than they were, but she wouldn't cheat. She'd been cheated on, so had he, and they both knew how awful it made the other person feel. How could he believe that she was capable of inflicting such pain?

She got it, she did. She understood how much it had to have hurt to be so betrayed by Ben and Kelly and she understood why he shied away from any feelings of intimacy. She understood his reluctance to trust her, but it still slayed her that Ryan didn't seem to know her at all. How could he believe that she would do that, that she would hurt him that way after everything they'd both experienced? Didn't he have the faintest inkling that she loved him? How could he be so blind?

"I'm so sorry, Jaci," Shona said and Jaci blinked at her friend's statement. She'd totally forgotten that she was there. "Are you going back to London?"

Jaci lifted her shoulders in a slow shrug. "I'm not sure."

"Sorry again." Shona squeezed her shoulder before walking back to her desk.

So was she, Jaci thought. But she couldn't make someone love her. Her feelings were her own and she couldn't project them onto Ryan. She could, maybe, forgive his verbal attack in the driveway of Lyon House, but by ignoring her he'd shown her that he regretted sharing his past with her, that he didn't trust her and, clearly, that he did not want to pursue a relationship with her. It hurt like open-heart surgery but she could deal with it, she *would* deal with it. She was never going to be the person who loved too much, who demanded too much, who gave too much, again.

When she loved again, *if* she ever loved again, it would be on her terms. She would never settle for anything less than amazing again. She wanted to be someone's sanctuary, her lover's soft place to fall. She wanted to be the keeper of his secrets and, harder, the person he confided his fears to. She wanted to be someone's everything.

Walking away from another relationship, from this situation that was rapidly turning toxic, wasn't an easy decision to make, but she knew that it was the right path. It didn't matter that it was hard, that she felt the brutal sting of loss and disappointment. She couldn't allow it to dictate her life. She was stronger and braver and more resilient than she'd ever been, and she wouldn't let this push her back into being that weak, insecure girl she'd been before.

It was time that she started protecting her heart, her feelings and her soul. It was time, as her mum had suggested, to stop standing and start walking.

Because he'd spent the past week chasing down old contacts and new leads, Ryan quickly realized that there was no money floating around to finance *Blown Away*. *We're in a recession, we don't have that much, it's too risky, credit is tight.* He'd heard the same excuses time and time again.

This was the end of the line. He was out of options.

Not quite true, he reluctantly admitted. He still had his father's offer to finance a movie, but he'd rather wash his face with acid than ask him. He could always come back to *Blown Away* in the future, but Jaci's career would take a hit...

Jaci... No, he wasn't going to think about her at all. It was over and she had—according to the very brief letter she'd left with his PA—released him from her contract.

She was out of his life, and that was good. But his mind kept playing the last scenes of their movie in his head. Instead of fighting the memory, as he had been doing, instead of pushing it aside, he let it run. It wasn't as if he was doing any work, and maybe if he just remembered, properly, the events of that night, he'd be able to move *on*. He *had* to get his life back to normal.

He remembered the wedding, how amazing Jaci looked in that pale pink cocktail dress with the straps that crisscrossed her back. Her eyes looked deep and mysterious and her lips had been painted a color that matched her dress. He'd kept his eyes on her all night, had followed her progress across the tented room, watched her talk to friends and acquaintances, noticed how she refused the many offers to dance. After the meal, the horse's ass had approached her and she'd looked wary and distant. They'd talked and talked and Clive kept moving closer and Jaci kept putting distance between them.

Ryan frowned. She *had* done that. He wasn't imagining that. Clive had eventually left her, looking less than happy. Then he'd joined her at that table and they'd chatted and the pinched look left her eyes. Her attention had been on him, all on him; her eyes softened when they looked at *him*. Her entire attention had been focused on him; she hadn't looked around. Clive had been forgotten when they were together.

She'd been that into me...

So how had she gone from being so into him to jumping into bed with Whips? *Did she? Are you so sure that she did?* Ryan picked up his pen and tapped it against his desk. He had no proof that Jaci had slept with Clive, just his notoriously unreliable gut instinct. And his intuition was clouded by jealously and past insecurities about being cheated on...

He wished he could talk to someone who would tell him the unvarnished, dirty truth.

Jaci's ball-breaker sister would do that. Merry had never pulled her punches. Ryan picked up his mobile and within a minute Meredith's cut-glass tones swirled around his office. "Are you there, you ridiculous excuse for a human being?"

Whoa! Someone sounded very irritated with him. That was okay because he was still massively irritated with her sister. "Did she sleep with Whips and Chains?" he demanded.

"We video chatted last night and she looked like death warmed up. I have never seen her so unhappy, so…so… so heartbroken. She cries herself to sleep every night, Ryan, did you know that?"

Ryan's heart lurched. "Did. She. Sleep. With. Him?"

There was a long, intense silence on the other end of the phone and Ryan pulled the receiver away, looked at it and spoke into it again. "Are you there?"

"Oh, dear Lord in heaven," Merry stated on a long sigh. Her voice lost about 50 percent of its tartness when she spoke again. "Ryan Jackson, why would you think that Jaci slept with Clive?"

"That morning she looked…" Ryan felt as if his head was about to explode. "… God, I don't know. She… glowed. She looked like something wonderful had happened. Your dad told me that they were in her bedroom so I presumed that they'd…reconciled."

"You are an idiot of magnificent proportions," Merry told him, exasperated. "Now, listen to me, birdbrain. Clive came to pick up some stuff of his she was storing at Lyon House. That's the only reason he was there. Yes, she told him about New York, how happy she was there.

Because she's a girl and she has her pride, she wanted
Clive to know how happy and successful she was, how
much she didn't need him. She told Clive about Banks,
and you, because she wanted to show him that there were
other men out there, rich, powerful and successful men,
who wanted and desired her. She wanted him to know
that she didn't need him anymore because she was now
a better version of who she used to be with him."

Ryan struggled to keep up. "She told you all that?"

"Yeah. She's proud of who she is now, Ryan, proud
of the fact that she picked herself up and dusted herself
off. Sure, she should never have told Clive what she did
but she never thought that he would talk to the press...
I would've suspected him but she's not cynical like me.
Or you."

"I'm not cynical," Ryan objected but he knew that he
was. Of course he was.

Merry snorted. "Sure, you are. You thought Jaci slept
with her ex because she looked *happy*. Anyway, Jaci
blames herself for you losing the funding. She blames
herself for all of it. Her dream is gone, Ryan."

He'd made a point of not thinking about that because
if he did, it hurt too damn much. He rubbed his eyes with
his index finger and thumb. "I know."

"But worse than that, she's shattered that you could
think that she slept with Clive, that she would cheat on
you. She feels annihilated because she never believed
that you could think that of her."

Ryan rested his elbow on his desk and pushed the ball
of his hand into his temple. He felt as if the floor had
fallen out from under his feet. "Oh." It was the only word
he could articulate at the moment.

"Fix this, Jackson," Merry stated in a low voice that was superscary. "Or I swear I'll hurt you."

He could do that, Ryan thought, sucking in air. He could...he could fix this. He *had* to fix this. Because Jaci had been hurt and no one, especially not him, was allowed to do that.

The fact that Merry would—actually—hurt him was just an added incentive.

There was only one person in the world whom he would do this for, Ryan thought, as the front door to Chad's house opened and his father stood in the doorway with an openly surprised look on his face.

Ryan held his father's eyes and fought the urge to leave. He reminded himself that this was for Jaci, this was to get her the big break that she so richly deserved. Shelving *Blown Away* meant postponing Jaci's dream. He couldn't do that to her. Once the world and, more important, other producers saw the quality of her writing, she'd have more work than she could cope with and she'd be in demand, and maybe then they could find a way to be together. Because, God, he missed her.

He loved her, he needed her, and there was no way that he could return to her—to beg her to take him back—without doing everything and anything he could to resurrect her dream. She'd probably tell him to go to hell, and he suspected that he had as much chance of getting her back as he did of having sex with a zombie princess, but he had to try. Writing made her happy and, above all, he wanted her happy.

With or without him.

"Are you going to stand there and stare at me or are

you going to come in?" Chad asked, that famous smile hovering around his lips.

Yeah, he supposed he should. Bombshells shouldn't be dropped on front porches, especially a porch as magnificent as this one. Ryan walked inside the hall and looked around; nothing much had changed since the last time he was here. What was different, and a massive surprise, was the large framed photograph of Ben and himself, arms draped around each other's shoulders, wearing identical grins, that stood on a hall table. Well…huh.

"Do you want to talk in the study or by the pool?" Chad asked.

Ryan pushed his hand through his hair. "Study, I guess." He followed his father down the long hallway of the sun-filled home, catching glances of the magnificent views of the California coastline through the open doors of the rooms they passed. He might not love his father, but he'd always loved this house.

Chad opened the door to the study and gestured Ryan to a chair. "Do you want a cup of coffee?"

Ryan could see that Chad expected him to refuse but he was exhausted, punch-drunk from not sleeping for too many nights. He needed caffeine so he quickly accepted. Chad called his housekeeper on the intercom, asked for coffee and sat down in a big chair across the desk from him. "So, what's this about, Ryan? Or should I call you Jax?"

"Ryan will do." Ryan pulled out a sheaf of papers from his briefcase and slapped them on the table. "According to the emails you've sent me in the past, you are part of a group prepared to invest in my films. I'd like to know whether you, and your consortium, would like to invest in *Blown Away*."

Chad looked at him for a long time before slowly nodding. "Yes," he eventually stated, quietly and without any fanfare.

"I need a hundred million."

"You could have more if you need it."

"That'll do." Ryan felt the pure, clean feeling of relief flood through him, and he slumped back in his chair, suddenly feeling energized. It had been a lot easier than he expected, he thought. He was prepared to grovel, to beg if he needed to. Asking his father for the money had stung a lot less than he expected it to. Because Jaci, and her happiness, was a lot more important to him than his pride.

It was that simple.

"That's it? Just like that?" Ryan thought he should make sure that his father didn't have anything up his sleeve, a trick that could come back and bite him on the ass.

Chad linked his hands across his flat stomach and shrugged. "An explanation would be nice but it's not a deal breaker. I know that you'd rather swallow nails than ask me for help, so it has to be a hell of a story."

Ryan jumped to his feet and walked over to the open door that led onto a small balcony and sucked in the fragrant air. He rested his shoulder against the doorjamb and looked at his father. In a few words he explained about Banks and Jaci's part in the fiasco. "But, at the end of the day, it was my fault. Who risks a hundred million dollars by having a pretend relationship with a woman?"

"Someone who desperately wanted a relationship but who was too damn scared to admit it and used any excuse he could to have one anyway?"

Bull's-eye, Father. Bull's-eye. He had been scared and stupid. But mostly scared. Scared of falling in love, of trusting someone, terrified of being happy. Then scared of being miserable. But hey, he was miserable anyway, and wasn't that a kick in the pants?

"As glad as I am that you've asked me to help, I would've thought that you'd rather take a hit on the movie than come to me," Chad commented, and Ryan, from habit, looked for the criticism in his words but found none. Huh. He was just sitting there, head cocked, offering his help and not looking for a fight. What had happened to his father?

"Why are you being so nice about this?" he demanded. "This isn't like you."

Chad flushed. With embarrassment? That was also new. "It isn't like the person I used to be. Losing Ben made me take a long, hard look at myself, and I didn't like what I saw. Since then I've been trying to talk to you to make amends."

Now, that was pushing the feasibility envelope. "And you did that by demanding ten million for narrating the documentary about Ben's life?" He shot the words out and was glad that his voice sounded harsh. Anger he could deal with, since he was used to fighting with his father.

Chad didn't retaliate and he remained calm. A knock on the door broke the tension and he turned to see Chad's housekeeper in the doorway, carrying a tray holding a carafe and mugs. She placed it on his desk, smiled when Chad politely thanked her and left the room. Chad, ignoring Ryan's outburst, poured him a cup and brought it over to him.

Ryan took the mug and immediately lifted the cup to his lips, enjoying the rich taste. He needed to get out of this room, needed to get back to business. He gestured to the contract. "There's the deal. Get it to your lawyers but tell them that they need to get cracking. I don't have a lot of time."

"All right." Chad nodded. "Let's go back a step and talk about that demand I made for payment for narrating that movie."

"We don't have to… What's done is done."

"It really isn't," Chad replied. His next question was one Ryan didn't expect. "Did you want to do that documentary? I know that Ben's friends were asking you to, that you were expected to."

God, how was he supposed to answer that? If he said yes, he'd be lying—the last thing he'd wanted at the time was to do a movie about his brother, who died on his way back from a dirty weekend with his fiancée—and if he said no then Chad would want an explanation as to why not. "I don't want to talk about this."

"Tough. I think it's time that you understood that I made that demand so that you couldn't do the movie… to give you an out."

Ryan frowned, disconcerted. Chad jammed his hands into the pockets of his shorts and looked Ryan in the eye. "I knew that Ben was fooling around with Kelly and I told him to stop. It wasn't appropriate and I didn't approve. You didn't deserve that amount of disloyalty, especially not from Ben."

Chad's words were like a fist to his stomach, and he couldn't get enough air to his brain to make sense of his statements. "What?"

"Ben told me that they were just scratching an itch and I told him to scratch it with someone else. He promised me that that weekend would be the last time, that they'd call it off when they got back. I wanted to warn you about marrying her but I knew that you wouldn't have listened to me."

"I wouldn't have," Ryan agreed. He and Chad had been at odds long before the accident.

Chad dropped his eyes. "My fault. I was a useless father and terrible role model. I played with women and didn't take them seriously. Ben followed my example." He walked back to his desk, poured coffee into his own cup and sipped. "Anyway, to come back to the documentary… I knew that asking you to make that film would've been cruel so I made damn sure that the project got scuttled."

Ryan wished he could clear the cobwebs from his head. "By asking for that ridiculous fee."

"Yeah. I knew that you didn't have the cash, that you wouldn't borrow the money to do it and that you wouldn't ask anyone else to narrate it." Chad shrugged. "That being said, I still have the script and if you ever want to take on the project, I'll narrate it, for free."

Ryan slid down the door frame to sink to his haunches. "God." He looked up. "I came to ask you for a hundred million and I end up feeling totally floored."

Chad rubbed the back of his neck. "Neither you nor your mother deserved any of the pain I put you through. I've been trying to find a way to say I'm sorry for years." His jaw set and he looked like the stubborn, selfish man whom Ryan was used to. "And if I have to spend a hundred million to do it then I will." He grabbed the stack of papers, flipped to the end page and reached for a pen. Ryan watched, astounded, as he dashed his signature across the page.

"Don't you have to talk to your partners?" Ryan asked.

"I'm the only investor," Chad said, quickly initialing the pages.

Well, okay, then. "Don't you think your lawyers should read the contract or, at the very least, that you should?" Ryan asked as he stood up, now feeling slightly bemused. He was still trying to work through the fact that his father had been trying to protect him from further hurt, that Chad seemed to want a relationship with him, that it seemed as if his father had, to some measure, changed.

"No, no lawyers. We'll settle this now and before you leave town I'll do a direct deposit into your account for half of the cash. I'll need some time to get you the other half. A week, maybe. Besides, if you take me for a hundred million then it's no less than what I deserve for being the worst father in the world."

Ryan picked his jaw up from the floor. "Chad, hell... I don't know what to say."

"Say that you'll consider me for a part in the movie... any part," Chad retorted, as quick as lightning.

Ryan had to laugh and felt strangely relieved knowing that his father hadn't undergone a total personality change.

"I'll consider it."

Chad lifted his head and flashed him a smile. "That's my boy."

Twelve

In all honesty, Jaci was proud of her heart. It had been kicked, battered, punched, stabbed and pretty much broken but it still worked…sort of, kind of. It still pumped blood around her body but, on the downside, it still craved Ryan, missed him with every beat.

This was the height of folly because his silence over the past ten days had just reinforced her belief that he'd been playing with her, possibly playing her. If he felt anything for her, apart from sex, he would've contacted her long before this, but he hadn't and that was that.

Ryan aside, she had other problems to deal with. Her career as a screenwriter was on the skids and there was absolutely nothing she could do about that. Before she'd left Starfish the office rumors had been flying, and even if she took only 5 percent of what was being said as truth, then she knew that there was more chance of the world ending this month than there was of *Blown Away* reaching the moviegoing public. And with that went her big break, her career as a screenwriter. She would have to start again with another script and see if her agent could get lucky a second time around. She wasn't holding her breath...

Being the scriptwriter for a blockbuster like *Blown Away*—and it would have been a blockbuster, of that she had no doubt—would have got her noticed and she would have been on her way to the success that she'd always craved.

She didn't crave it so much anymore. Since her conversation with her mother and Merry on the terrace at Lyon House, the desire to prove herself to her family, to herself, had dissipated. She knew that she was a good writer, and if it took another ten years for her to sell a script, she'd keep writing because this was what she was meant to do. This was what made her happy, and writing scripts was what she was determined to stick with. She'd keep on truckin' and one day, someday, her script would see the big screen.

It was wonderfully liberating to be free of that choking need to prove herself... She was Jaci and she was enough. And if that stupid, moron man couldn't see that, then he was a stupid moron man.

And who was leaning on her doorbell at eleven thirty at night? What was so important that it couldn't wait until morning?

Jaci hauled herself to her feet and walked to her door. When she pressed the intercom button and asked who was there, there was silence. Yay, now she had a creepoid pressing random doorbells. Well, they could carry on. She was going to bed, where she was determined to not think about stupid men in general and a moronic man in particular.

A hard rap had her spinning around, and she glared at her door. Frowning, she walked back to the door and looked through the peephole and gasped when she saw Ryan's distorted face on the other side. Now he wanted to talk to her? Late at night when she was just dressed in a rugby jersey of Neil's that she'd liberated a decade ago, fuzzy socks and crazy hair? Was he insane?

"Let me in, Jace."

At the sound of his voice, her traitorous heart did a long, slow, happy slide from one side of her rib cage to the other. Stupid thing. "No."

"Come on, Jaci, we need to talk." Ryan's voice floated under the door.

Jaci, forgetting that she looked like an extra in a vampire movie, jerked the door open and slapped her hands on her hips. She shot him a look that was hot and frustrated. "Go away. Go far, far away!"

Ryan pushed her back into her apartment, shut the door behind him and shrugged out of his leather jacket. Despite her anger, and her disappointment, Jaci noticed that Ryan looked exhausted. He had twin blue-black stripes under his eyes and he looked pale. So their time apart hadn't been easy on him, either, she realized, and she was human enough to feel a tiny bit vindicated about that. But she also wanted to pull him into her arms, to soothe away his pain.

She loved him, and always would. Dammit.

Jaci slapped her hands across her chest. "What do you want, Ryan?"

Ryan shoved his hands into the front pockets of his

jeans and rocked on his heels. "I came to tell you that I've secured another source of funding for *Blown Away*."

Really? Oh, goodie! Jaci realized that he couldn't hear her sarcastic thoughts, so she glared at him again. "*That's* why you're here?"

Ryan looked confused. "Well, yeah. I thought you'd be pleased."

Jaci brushed past him, yanked her door open and waved her arm to get him to walk out. When he didn't, she pushed the words through her gritted teeth. "Get out."

"The funding isn't from Banks, it's from…" he hesitated for a moment before shaking his head. "…someone else."

"I don't care if it's from the goblins under the nearest bridge."

"Jaci, what the hell? This is your big break. This is what you wanted." Ryan looked utterly confused and more than a little irate. "I've been busting my ass to sort this out, and this is your response?"

"Did I ask you to?" Jaci demanded. "Did I ask you to roar off, ignore me for days, refuse to take my calls and keep me in the dark?"

"Look, maybe I should've called—"

"Maybe?" Jaci kicked the door shut with her foot and slapped her hands on his chest, attempting and failing to push him back. "Damn right you should've called! You don't get to fall in and out of my life. I'm not a doll you can pick up and discard on a whim."

"No, you're just an enormous pain in my ass." Ryan captured her wrists with one hand and gripped her hip with his other hand, pulling her into his rock-hard erection. "You drive me mad, you're on my mind first thing in the morning and last thing at night and, annoyingly, pretty much any minute in between." He dropped his mouth onto hers and slid his tongue between her lips. Jaci felt her joints melt and tried not to sink into him. He was like the worst street drug she could imagine—one hit and she was addicted all over again.

She felt Ryan's hands slide up her waist to cover her breasts and she shuddered. One more time, one more memory. She needed it and she needed him.

One more time and then she'd kick him out. Of her apartment and her life.

"There you are," Ryan murmured against her mouth. "I needed you back in my arms."

He needed *her*? Back in his arms? Oh, God, he wasn't back because he loved her or missed her. He was back because he loved the sex and he missed it. Stiffening, she pulled her mouth from his and narrowed her eyes. "Back off," she muttered.

Ryan lifted his hands and took a half step away. He ran a hand around the back of his neck and blew air into his cheeks. "Jace, I—"

Jaci shook her head and pushed past him, thinking that she needed some distance, just a moment to get her heart and head under control. She walked into the bathroom and gripped the edge of the sink, telling herself that she had to resist temptation because she couldn't kid herself anymore; Ryan wanted to have sex and she wanted to make love. Settling for less than she wanted wasn't an option anymore. She didn't want to settle for a bouquet of flowers when she needed the whole damn florist. Jaci placed her elbows on the bathroom counter and stared at her pale reflection in the mirror.

She needed more and she had to tell him. It was that simple. And that hard. She'd tell him that she loved him and he'd walk, because he wasn't interested in anything that even hinted at permanence.

Her expiration date was up.

"You can do this, you are stronger than you think." Jaci whispered the words to herself.

"You can do what?"

Jaci stood up and slowly turned around to Ryan standing in the entrance to the bathroom, holding the top rim of the door. He looked hot and sexy and rumpled. Still tired, she thought, but so damn confident. God, she needed every bit of willpower she possessed to walk away from him, but if she didn't do it now she never would.

Jaci pulled in a deep breath. "I'm walking away… from you, from this."

Ryan tipped his head to the side and Jaci saw the corners of his mouth twitch in amusement. Ooh, that look made her want to smack him silly.

"No," he calmly stated. He dropped his hands and crossed his arms over that ocean of a chest and spread his legs, effectively blocking her path out of the bathroom.

That just made her mad. "What do you mean *no*? I am going to leave New York and I am definitely leaving you."

"No, you are not leaving New York and you are definitely not leaving me."

Jaci leaned back against the counter and thought that it was ridiculous that they were having this conversation in the bathroom. "I refuse to be your part-time plaything."

"You're not my plaything and, judging by the space you take up in my head, you're not a part-time anything."

"You run, Ryan. Every time I need you to talk to me, you run," Jaci cried.

To her surprise, he nodded his agreement. "Because you scare me. You scare the crap out of me."

"Why?" Jaci wailed, not understanding any of it.

Ryan lifted one powerful shoulder in a long shrug. "Because I'm in love with you."

No, he wasn't. He *couldn't* be. "You're not in love with me," Jaci told him, her voice shaky. "People in love don't act like you did. They don't accuse people of having affairs. They don't try to hurt the people they love!"

Horror chased pain and regret across his face. "Sorry. God, I'm so sorry that I hurt you," Ryan said in a strangled voice. "I'd just heard that you discussed us with that horse's butt and you looked all dewy, and soft, and in love. I thought that you'd gone back to him."

"Why did you think that?"

"Because it's the way you look after I make love to you!" Ryan shouted, his chest heaving. "I was jealous and scared and I didn't want to be in love with you, to expose myself to being hurt. You loved him three months ago, Jaci."

"That was before I learned that he liked S&M and that he cheated on me. It was before I grew stronger, bolder. It was before I met you. How could you think that, Ryan? How could you believe that I would hurt you like that?"

"Because I'm scared to love you, to be with you." Ryan's jaw was rock hard and his eyes were bleak. When he spoke again, his words sounded as if he was chipping them from a mound of granite. "Because all the people who I loved have let me down in some way or the other. I love you, and why would life treat me any different now?" He shrugged and he swallowed, emotion making his Adam's apple bounce in his strong throat. "But I'm willing to take the chance. You're that important."

No, he wasn't, and he couldn't be in love with her. It sounded far too good to be true.

"You don't love me," Jaci insisted, her voice shaky.

Yet she could hear, and she was sure he could, too, the note of hope in her voice.

"Yeah, I do. I am so in love with you. I didn't want to be, didn't think I ever would fall in love again, but I have. With you." He didn't touch her, he didn't try to persuade her with his body because his eyes, his fabulous eyes, radiated the truth of that statement. He loved her? Good grief. Jaci gripped the counter with her hands in an effort to keep from hurtling herself into his arms.

"But you run, every time. Every time we get close, you bolt."

"And that's something I will try to stop doing," Ryan told her, a smile starting to flirt with his eyes and mouth. He held out his broad hand to her and waited until she placed hers in it. Jaci sighed at the warmth of his fingers curling around hers. She stared down at their intertwined hands and wondered if she was dreaming. But if she was, surely she would've chosen a more romantic setting for this crazy conversation? It was a tiny bathroom in a tiny apartment... It didn't matter, she'd take it. She'd take him.

Ryan's finger under her chin lifted her face up and she gasped at the love she saw in his eyes. No, this was too good to be a dream. "I really don't want to carry on this conversation in the bathroom, but you're not getting out of here before I hear what I need to."

Jaci grinned and picked up her spare hand and ran her finger over his collarbone, down his chest, across those ridges in his abdomen, stopping very low down. "What do you want to hear? That I love your body? I do," she teased and saw his eyes darken with passion.

Ryan gripped her finger to stop it going lower. "You know what I want to hear, Jace. Tell me."

When Jaci saw the emotion in his eyes, all thoughts

of teasing him evaporated. He looked unsure and a little scared. As if he was expecting her to reject him, to reject them. Her heart, bottom lip and hands trembled from excitement, from love…

"Ryan, of course I love you. I have for a while."

Ryan rested his forehead on hers and she could feel the tension leaving his body. "Thank God."

"How could you not know that?" Jaci linked her arms around his neck and placed her face against his strong chest. "Honestly, for a smart man you can be such an idiot on occasion."

"Apparently so," Ryan agreed, his arms holding her tightly. He pulled his head back to smile at her, relief and passion and, yes, love dancing in his eyes. "Come back to bed, darling, and let me show you how much I love and adore you."

"You've just missed sex," Jaci teased him on a happy laugh.

Ryan pushed her bangs off her forehead and rubbed the pad of his thumb across her delicately arched brow. "No, sweetheart, I've just missed you." He grinned. "But hey, I'm a guy, and if you're offering…"

Jaci launched herself upward and he caught her as she wrapped her legs around his waist. "Anywhere, anyhow, anytime."

Ryan kissed her open mouth, and Jaci's body sighed and shivered in anticipation. "Can I add that to your contract?" he asked as he backed out of the bathroom into the bedroom.

Lover, friend, boss…there wasn't much she wouldn't do for him, Jaci thought as he lowered her onto the bed and covered her body with his.

Anything. Anywhere. Anytime.

* * *

Much, much later Ryan was back in his jeans and Jaci was wearing his button-down shirt and they were sitting cross-legged on her bed, digging chocolate chip ice cream from the container she'd abandoned earlier.

What an evening, Jaci thought, casting her mind back over the past few hours. She felt as if she'd ridden a crazy roller coaster of emotion, stomach churning, heart thumping adrenaline, and she'd come out the other side thrilled. Happy. Content. Dopey. Oh, they still had a lot to talk about, but they'd be fine.

Had he really said that he'd secured funding for *Blown Away*? Her spoon stopped halfway to her mouth and she didn't realize that ice cream was rolling off the utensil and dropping to her knee. "Did I hear you say that you have funding for *Blown Away*?"

Ryan leaned forward, maneuvered the spoon in her hand to his mouth and ran his thumb over the ice cream on her knee, licking his digit afterward. "Uh-huh."

"Do I have to pretend to be your girlfriend or your wife this time?" Jaci teased.

"No pretending needed this time," Ryan said, peering into the empty container. "Is that it? Damn! I'm still starving. Don't you have any real food in this house?"

"No, I was on the I-hate-men diet. Ice cream and wine only." Jaci tossed her spoon into the container and placed her elbows on her knees. "Who is your investor, Ry? Did you make nice with Banks?"

"Hell no! However, I did meet with him. I felt I owed him that."

"And?"

"He ripped into me, which I expected. Afterwards

he offered me half of the money, told me that he wanted you off the project and that he wanted creative control."

"And you said no. You'd never give him control."

Ryan sent another longing look at the empty ice cream container. "That was part of it but not having you as part of the project was the deal breaker. I need real food."

He was trying to change the subject, Jaci realized. *No chance, buddy.* "Ok, so who is this new investor that you found so quickly?"

Ryan stretched his legs out and placed them on each side of her hips. He leaned forward and dropped his head to nibble on her exposed collarbone. Jaci frowned, pushed his head away and leaned back so that she could see his face. "Stop trying to distract me, Jackson, and keep talking to me."

Ryan twisted his lips and tipped his face up so that he was looking at the ceiling. Okay, it didn't take a rocket scientist to realize that he didn't want to talk about this, but the sooner he learned that she was the one person he could talk to, the easier the process would get.

"Chad Bradshaw," he reluctantly admitted.

Jaci gasped. "What? Chad? Your father?"

"You know any other Chad Bradshaw?" Ryan muttered.

Jaci rubbed her forehead with the tips of her fingers. "Wait, hold on a second, let me catch up. Your father, the father you don't talk to, is financing your movie?"

"Yep."

Oh, right, so she was going to have to drag this out of him. Well, she would, if she had to. "Ryan, we're in a relationship, right?"

Ryan smiled and it warmed every strand of DNA in her body. "Damn straight," he replied.

"Okay, then, well, that means that we get to have spectacular sex—" Jaci glanced at her messy bed and nodded "—check that—and that we talk to each other. So talk. Now."

"I went to go see him," Ryan eventually admitted in a low voice. "I needed the money, I knew that he wanted to invest in one of my projects, so I made it happen."

That didn't explain a damn thing. "But why? You told me that if Banks bailed, you would mothball *Blown Away*."

Ryan squeezed her hips with the insides of his calves. "My and Thom's careers would withstand the hit, but yours wouldn't."

It took a minute for her to make sense of those words, and when she did, she tumbled a little deeper and a little further into love. She hadn't thought it possible, but this was just another surprise in a night full of them. "But you hate your father."

"Well, *hate* is a strong word." He pulled his long legs up and rested his elbows on his knees. "Look, Jace, the reality is that your career is on a knife's edge. Your script is stunning but if nobody sees your work, it could be months, years before you get another shot at the big leagues. I don't want you to have to wait years for another chance, so I made it happen."

Jaci placed her hands on his strong forearms and rested her forehead on her wrists. "Oh, Ryan, you do love me."

His fingers tunneled into her hair. "Yep. An amazing amount, actually."

Jaci's heart sighed. She lifted her head and pulled back. "Did he make you grovel?"

Ryan shook his head. "He was…pretty damn cool, actually." Ryan took a deep breath and Jaci listened intently as he explained how Chad had known about Ben's affair with Kelly and how Chad had clumsily, Jaci thought, tried to protect Ryan. It was so Hollywood, so messed up, but sweet nonetheless.

"Chad tried to explain that they, Ben and Kelly and Chad himself, looked at affairs differently than I did. That to them sex was just sex, an itch to scratch, I think he said. That they didn't mean to hurt me."

"It shouldn't have mattered how they felt about sex. They knew how you felt and they should've taken that into account," Jaci said, her voice hot. She looked at Ryan's bemused face and reined her temper in. "Sorry, sorry, it just makes me so angry when excuses are made."

"I've never had anyone defend me before."

"Well, just so you know, I'll always be in your corner, fists up and prepared to fight for you," Jaci told him, ignoring the sheen of emotion in his eyes. Her big, tough warrior-like man...emotional? He'd hate her to comment on it so she moved the conversation along briskly. "What else did Chad have to say?"

"That he would narrate the documentary on Ben if I ever chose to do it. For free this time. But I don't know if I can make that film."

"You'll know when you're ready."

Ryan's hand gripped her thigh. "It's not because I care about their affair or care about her anymore, Jace. You understand that, don't you? It feels like another life, another time, and I'm ready to move on, with you. It's just that he was..."

"Your hero. Your brother, your best friend." Jaci touched his cheek with her fingertips. "Honey, there is no rule that you have to make a movie on him. Maybe you should remember him like you'd like to remember him and let everyone else do the same."

Ryan placed his hand on top of hers and held it to his cheek. He closed his eyes and Jaci looked at him, her masculine, strong, flawed man. God, she loved him. She saw his Adam's apple bob and knew that he was fighting to keep his emotions from bubbling up and over.

"Don't, Ry, don't hide what you're feeling from me," she told him, her voice low. "I know talking about Ben hurts. I'm sorry."

Ryan jerked his head up and his eyes blazed with heat, and hope, and love. "I'm not thinking about him. I'm thinking about you and us and this bright new life we have in front of us. I'm so damn happy, Jace. You make me."

Jaci cocked her head. "You make me...what?"

"That's all. You just make me."

Jaci sighed as he kissed the center of her palm and placed her hand on his heart. "I never realized how alone I was until you hurtled into my life. You've put color into my world, and I promise I'll make you happy, Jace."

Jaci blinked away her happy tears. "For how long?" she whispered.

Ryan pushed her long bangs out of her eyes and tucked them behind her ear. "Forever...if you'll let me."

Jaci leaned in for a kiss and smiled against his mouth. "Oh, Ry, I think we can do better than that. Amazing love stories last longer than that."

* * * * *

*If you loved TAKING THE BOSS TO BED
by Joss Wood, pick up these other stories about
sexy bosses from Harlequin Desire!*

*COURTING THE COWBOY BOSS
by USA TODAY bestselling author Janice Maynard*

*MINDING HER BOSS'S BUSINESS
by USA TODAY bestselling author Janice Maynard*

*BEGUILING THE BOSS
by New York Times bestselling author Joan Hohl*

*HAVING HER BOSS'S BABY
by USA TODAY bestselling author Maureen Child*

*NOT THE BOSS'S BABY
by Sarah M. Anderson*

Available now from Harlequin Desire!

***

*If you're on Twitter, tell us what you think of
Harlequin Desire! #harlequindesire*

COMING NEXT MONTH FROM

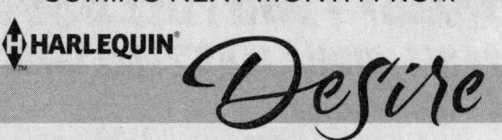

Available January 5, 2016

#2419 TWIN HEIRS TO HIS THRONE
Billionaires and Babies • by Olivia Gates
Prince Voronov disappeared after he broke Kassandra's heart, leaving her pregnant and alone. Now the future king has returned to claim his twin heirs. Will he reclaim Kassandra's heart as part of the bargain?

#2420 NANNY MAKES THREE
Texas Cattleman's Club: Lies and Lullabies
by Cat Schield
Hadley Stratton is more than the nanny Liam Ward hired for his unexpected newborn niece. She's also the girl who got away...and the rich rancher is not going to let that happen twice!

#2421 A BABY FOR THE BOSS
Pregnant by the Boss • by Maureen Child
Is his one-time fling and current employee guilty of corporate espionage? Billionaire boss Mike Ryan believes so, but he'll need to reevaluate everything when he learns she's carrying his child...

#2422 PREGNANT BY THE RIVAL CEO
by Karen Booth
Anna Langford wants the deal—even though it means working with the guy she's never forgotten. But what starts as business turns into romance—until Anna learns of Jacob's ruthless motives and her unplanned pregnancy!

#2423 THAT NIGHT WITH THE RICH RANCHER
Lone Star Legends • by Sara Orwig
Tony can't believe the vision in red who won him at the bachelor auction. One night with Lindsay—his stubborn next-door neighbor—is all he'd signed up for. But her makeover has him forgetting all about their family feud!

#2424 TRAPPED WITH THE TYCOON
Mafia Moguls • by Jules Bennett
All that stands between mafia boss Braden O'Shea and what he wants is employee Zara Perkins. But when they're snowed in together, seduction becomes his only goal. Will he choose his family...or the woman he can't resist?

————

YOU CAN FIND MORE INFORMATION ON UPCOMING HARLEQUIN® TITLES, FREE EXCERPTS AND MORE AT WWW.HARLEQUIN.COM.

HDCNM1215

REQUEST YOUR FREE BOOKS!
2 FREE NOVELS PLUS 2 FREE GIFTS!

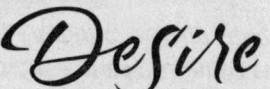

H HARLEQUIN®

Desire

ALWAYS POWERFUL, PASSIONATE AND PROVOCATIVE

YES! Please send me 2 FREE Harlequin® Desire novels and my 2 FREE gifts (gifts are worth about $10). After receiving them, if I don't wish to receive any more books, I can return the shipping statement marked "cancel." If I don't cancel, I will receive 6 brand-new novels every month and be billed just $4.55 per book in the U.S. or $5.24 per book in Canada. That's a savings of at least 13% off the cover price! It's quite a bargain! Shipping and handling is just 50¢ per book in the U.S. and 75¢ per book in Canada.* I understand that accepting the 2 free books and gifts places me under no obligation to buy anything. I can always return a shipment and cancel at any time. Even if I never buy another book, the two free books and gifts are mine to keep forever.

225/326 HDN GH2P

Name	(PLEASE PRINT)

Address		Apt. #

City	State/Prov.	Zip/Postal Code

Signature (if under 18, a parent or guardian must sign)

Mail to the **Reader Service:**
IN U.S.A.: P.O. Box 1867, Buffalo, NY 14240-1867
IN CANADA: P.O. Box 609, Fort Erie, Ontario L2A 5X3

Want to try two free books from another line?
Call 1-800-873-8635 or visit www.ReaderService.com.

* Terms and prices subject to change without notice. Prices do not include applicable taxes. Sales tax applicable in N.Y. Canadian residents will be charged applicable taxes. Offer not valid in Quebec. This offer is limited to one order per household. Not valid for current subscribers to Harlequin Desire books. All orders subject to credit approval. Credit or debit balances in a customer's account(s) may be offset by any other outstanding balance owed by or to the customer. Please allow 4 to 6 weeks for delivery. Offer available while quantities last.

Your Privacy—The Reader Service is committed to protecting your privacy. Our Privacy Policy is available online at www.ReaderService.com or upon request from the Reader Service.

We make a portion of our mailing list available to reputable third parties that offer products we believe may interest you. If you prefer that we not exchange your name with third parties, or if you wish to clarify or modify your communication preferences, please visit us at www.ReaderService.com/consumerchoice or write to us at Reader Service Preference Service, P.O. Box 9062, Buffalo, NY 14240-9062. Include your complete name and address.

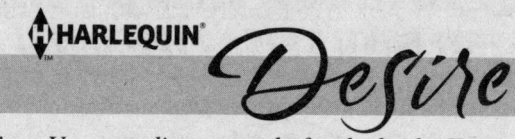
Kassandra fumbled for the remote, pushing every button before she managed to turn off the TV.

But it was too late. She'd seen him. For the first time since she'd walked out of his hospital room twenty-six months ago. That had been the last time the world had seen him, too. He'd dropped off the radar completely ever since. Now her retinas burned with the image of Leonid striding out of his imposing Fifth Avenue headquarters.

The man she'd known had been crackling with vitality, a smile of whimsy and assurance always hovering on his lips and sparkling in the depths of his eyes. This man was totally detached, as if he was no longer part of the world. Or as if it was beneath his notice. And there'd been another change. The stalking swagger was gone. In its place was a deliberate, almost menacing prowl.

This wasn't the man she'd known.

Or rather, the man she'd thought she'd known.

She'd long ago faced the fact that she'd known nothing of him. Not before she'd been with him, or while they'd been together, or after he'd shoved her away and vanished.

Kassandra had withdrawn from the world, too. She'd been pathetic enough to be literally sick with worry about him, to pine for him until she'd wasted away. Until she'd almost miscarried. That scare had finally jolted her to the one reality she'd been certain of. That she'd wanted that baby with everything in her and would never risk losing it. That day at the doctor's, she'd found out she wasn't carrying one baby, but two.

She'd reclaimed herself and her stability, had become even more successful career-wise, but most important, she'd become a mother to two perfect daughters. Eva and Zoya. She'd given them both names meaning life, as they'd given *her* new life.

Then Zorya had suddenly filled the news with a declaration of its intention to reinstate the monarchy. With every rapid development, foreboding had filled her. Even when she'd had no reason to think it would make Leonid resurface.

The doorbell rang.

It had become a ritual for her neighbor to come by and have a cup of tea so they could unwind together after their hectic days.

Rushing to the door, she opened it with a ready smile. "We should…"

Air clogged her lungs. All her nerves fired, short-circuiting her every muscle, especially her heart.

Leonid.

Right there. On her doorstep.

Don't miss TWIN HEIRS TO HS THRONE by USA TODAY bestselling author Olivia Gates, available January 2016 wherever Harlequin® Desire books and ebooks are sold.

www.Harlequin.com

HDEXP1215